Praise for *In These Five Breaths*

"*In These Five Breaths* is Paul Lipton's 'poem' to life in which each breath holds a promise of salvation, redemption, and forgiveness. Breath is a journey that the reader can take into a world we will enter sooner or later. Breath is a light into the beauty as the gift of each light. It lets us know that the quality of life is the compelling truth. Breath is light."
—**William Reichel, M.D.**, affiliated scholar, Center for Clinical Bioethics, Georgetown University Medical Center, Washington, D.C.

"In *In These Five Breaths*, Paul Lipton vividly describes our human experience. He beautifully illustrates the basic truth that too frequently eludes us: we only have this present moment—THIS BREATH—to live life with purpose and love. Life, Time, and Death are highlighted while Paul challenges the reader to live courageously in a world that leaves nobody unscathed. As a hospice physician, I see the story told in *In These Five Breaths* unfold every day with my patients and their families, which is why Paul's message deeply resonates within me. Paul Lipton is more than a gifted storyteller. He is a spiritual messenger that our world desperately needs right now. I invite you to read Paul's message."
—**Phil Ramos, M.D.**, board-certified nephrologist and Clinical Fellow, Harvard Palliative Care Fellowship Program 2018–2019

"If you have ever sat beside a loved one who is in the final stage of passing from this life and into eternity, as I have with both my mom and dad, then, like me, you likely wondered if, and probably hoped that they knew you were there with them on this journey. If so, then *In These Five Breaths* is a book you should read and meditate on as you contemplate the thoughts of both the one drawing his last few breaths and those who are there to comfort him."
—**Daniel E. Whiteman, Ph.D.**, Vice Chairman, Coastal Construction Company

"A beautiful, deeply authentic look at what really matters in a life when all the noise melts away. Give this book to anyone looking for meaning."
—**Jessie Hilb**, author of *The Calculus of Change*

In These Five Breaths

A Novel

Paul R. Lipton

Mulberry Harbor Press

Paul R. Lipton/Mulberry Harbor Press
Email: paulrlipton@gmail.com

Publisher's Note: This is a work of fiction. Names, characters, places, and incidents are a product of the author's imagination. Locales and public names are sometimes used for atmospheric purposes. Any resemblance to actual people, living or dead, or to businesses, companies, events, institutions, or locales is completely coincidental.

Cover design by Gus Yoo
Copy editing and book production by Stephanie Gunning
Book Layout © 2018 Book Design Templates

Library of Congress Control Number: 2018913108

In These Five Breaths/Paul R. Lipton. —1st ed.
ISBN 978-0-9890910-3-9 (paperback)

Contents

To Margie, Melissa, and Lindsay

"Life can only be understood backward, but it must be lived forward."

–SOREN KIERKEGAARD

God plays a trick on us, he thought. *God makes us live life forward, but it only makes sense backward.* This was one of the last thoughts he had as he took his last few breaths.

THE LOOK BACKWARD

There are a few breaths left. Maybe a few more than a few. Maybe five or six. Each one is forced. Each one is heavy. It is as if his body knows that it is winding down. At this moment, for some unknown reason, each breath is taking on a life of its own. His mind races over his life. Not from beginning to end but from end to beginning. It seems only to make sense backward.

How did he get here? The room is on the fifth floor of the community hospital. It is your typical hospital room. One bed, one TV, a small couch, and two metal chairs. And of course, all the tubes, wires, needles, lines, and related medical bells and whistles.

There are so many needles in him. There is a cast or two also. One cast is on an arm and one is on a leg. His leg in the cast is elevated by some mechanical gadget. There is an IV line that has a number of bags of fluid connected to it. Some of the bags are holding medicines of one sort or another and some are just for pain relief. He had been in a lot of pain but isn't anymore. There is just a dull throbbing feeling now. His body is numb. It feels like that feeling you have when you are coming out of a deep sleep.

There are at least two blankets on top of him and some type of compression socks. He must have been cold but he kind of feels nothing right now. He is oblivious to most senses at this point.

It is a Wednesday night. He has never thought he would die on a Wednesday, for some reason. He's always figured it would be a Sunday afternoon. A bright, shiny day. A cool breeze in the air. He had fantasized that it would be romantic. He thought it would be like in the movies, where he would be in an open field, looking healthy and handsome and saying something profound that would linger on people's minds for years, if not decades. You know, some witty, clever, imaginative insight on the meaning of life that would become the basis of a great religious revival or a classic poem, or perhaps a Russian romance novel.

Instead, it is a cold Wednesday night in a typical hospital room. Nothing romantic about it. Nothing memorable is going to happen here except that one more unimportant person will die. There is not a star in the sky. It is as close to bleak a scene as you could paint it.

How did this happen? His mind races. It was just two days ago that he was drinking coffee at the Brewing Market in Boulder. It was just off Canyon Boulevard. It was a usual Monday. Up at 6:30 A.M. Breakfast was some granola cereal and coffee. He'd checked his emails and text messages and then was off to the local CrossFit gym. After the hour and a half workout, it was another coffee at the coffee shop.

But here he is. Five breaths away from eternity. So, his mind continues the journey backward.

How did he get right here right now? He remembers being in a car. And that he felt a sharp pain. There was the mountain road. He remembers the car falling or tumbling or sliding. But how? What happened? It is all a blur.

Flashes of images roll by. All are scrambled like a badly made omelet.

Job choice.

School choice.

Work choice.

Friends made and lost.

Children.

His parents.

The tragedy that changed it all.

Dreams.

Nightmares.

And her. There was always her.

All these images, words, thoughts are flashing like neon signs in his mind.

Maybe at moments like these, you travel back in time and relive the moments that redirected you away from other options. Other choices. The *whys* and *how comes* of your life. It probably happens to all of us, though we rarely stop to reflect. But with five breaths left, it is happening to him.

The clock slows down. The pulse drops to its lowest reading ever. The heart rate winds down and the mind speeds up. Here he is, sixty-four years old. Not old in these days as compared to an earlier time. What is the saying . . . *Sixty is the new forty?* So, is sixty-four the new forty-four?

Boulder. Really. How did that happen? It was supposed to play out in Miami. That is where he practiced law for close to thirty years. Or was it supposed to play out in New York? That is where he grew up and had his first law job. Or was it supposed to play out in St. Louis? That is where he went to law school and had his first part-time law job after classes. Or was it supposed to play out in Paris, where he turned down a chance to totally redirect his life?

How does that happen? How do we choose? Truly life-changing decisions are so often made on a little more than a whim. Odd isn't it? We get married. Have children. Change jobs. Change cities. Pick up and move.

With each choice, our life and the lives of people we know and people we don't know yet are affected forever. And we all do that. Hundreds of times a day, if not more, we choose and the atoms in the air move, the wind shifts, the ripples in the stream of life set the butterfly effect in motion. That's where the flap of a butterfly wing in Cambodia causes a hurricane in the Atlantic.

What order should he travel in? Chronological? Life choices? Relationships? Loses? Deaths? Backward? Regrets? Mistakes? Loves?

He decides it must be relationships. After all, isn't that what happiness is all about? It really isn't the place. It really isn't the job. It always comes down to relationships. The ones who matter. The ones who enter your life and the ones who leave. What do you remember at moments like these? People! Love! Friends! Moments of joy and sadness. Moments of tragedy. Moments of grief.

And so, with the last five breaths of his life, he begins the journey. The journey back. Back so he can come to terms with now. He realizes that he has to solve the riddle of his life. Don't we all? Sooner or later we must come to terms with the *whys* and *what ifs,* so we can finally let go and be released.

Breath Five

He was home from school. It was December 1970. Not
the best of times in America due to the Vietnam War
and the protests. There were sit-ins and protest marches
on the college campuses. The Kent State shooting was
still on everyone's mind and the world seemed unsafe.
The country's traditional institutions were being
challenged.

How do you explain a country being ripped apart by
some politicians who are beholden to a few wealthy
donors or corporations? The average person was being
lost in the grab for money and power. *Maybe that is
always how it is,* he thinks. *Everyone goes on with their
day-to-day lives just trying to get by without the
government getting in their way.* You know . . . just
keep the streets paved, the lights working, and the
schools open . . . but otherwise stay out of our lives.

Yet, it didn't work that way. Frustrating indeed.

He was home from school halfway through his junior year at Penn State. It had been years since the assassinations of John and Martin and Bobby, yet things still felt off balance. Innocence seemed like a long-ago memory. The promise of a bright tomorrow seemed to have been shattered into a thousand different pieces. He longed for a return of innocence.

Maybe that is what attracted him to her when she first walked past him in a department store. They were both in from their respective schools. Home on Christmas break. She was in from the University of Cincinnati. A freshman. She was just so sweet- and innocent-looking. Kind of like stepping out of a charming children's bedtime story about a young girl lost in the big city. Big, clear eyes. A stance that said, "I am not certain what to do next but hope the world will be kind and won't treat me harshly." It was as if she was still maybe four or five years old and hiding behind her mom's skirt at the supermarket.

He was immediately attracted to her. It was a combination of her beauty, her natural innocence, the distant look in her eyes, and her evident kindness. She was just nice. But not nice in a boring way. Not nice in a yawning way. But rather, nice in a refreshing, wholesome, decent-person way. He fell hard right away.

It was as if his breathing stopped. But it hadn't.

The nurse comes in and checks his pulse. His wife holds his hand. She has done that a lot over the years. From that first meeting to now she has been by his side supporting him, holding his hand and encouraging him, even when he didn't deserve such devotion. It is just her nature. His mind races back again to their meeting and how the connection was sealed.

The department store was busy over the Christmas holidays. Back in 1970, there was no online shopping, so people would get in their cars, drive to the local downtown business district (there were no malls yet), find parking (usually free and on the street), and shop. It was an event. It was an afternoon or all-day affair. He was hired to play the guitar for customers as they wandered through the second floor, which included records and musical instruments. Vinyl records. When not strumming his guitar, he could choose which albums to play on the stereo. He usually chose the Beatles, or since it was the holiday season, *The Andy Williams Christmas Album*. There was a lot of "Silent Night" playing. He strummed the guitar to whatever was playing and sometimes turned off the vinyl and would play some Peter, Paul and Mary or Bob Dylan. Folk music was big at that time. Although it was a time of protests, they were protests with a Woody Guthrie slant; meaning, there was always a chanting of "This land belongs to all of us" and not just to the wealthy, powerful few.

She worked in the men's shoe department with other college girls who all were wearing college-style wardrobe supplied by the store. Basically, knee-high boots and short dresses or skirts with brightly colored sweaters. She was beyond cute, he thought, as he watched her on her breaks when she dropped by the music department to check out the new releases of albums and the young guitar player. It was all fun and innocent.

That word . . . *innocent* . . . seems to be ricocheting through his mind when he thinks of her and that time.

This is the way they met and how their journey together began. Her listening to him playing the guitar, small talk, flirting, and "How about a soda later?" type chat. And so, they began. Their dance would move across decades and many family and friend lifetimes and lead them to the highest joys and the deepest of sorrows.

He began to see the word *courage* flash through his mind. He coughed, and the nurse wiped the fluid from his mouth and nose.

How do we choose? How do we decide? What makes us introduce ourselves to one person over another? Turn left, not right? Ask for a phone number or not? What goes on inside each of us that triggers that reflect or action? It probably is a hundred or thousand different things that cause the motion. Instinct. Physical attraction. Emotional connection. Some link that you can't put your finger on. But there it is.

They connected that day. It could have just as easily been no connection at all if either had decided to simply grab lunch with someone else one day or not be in the mood for "a soda" when he asked her.

But once the connection was made, the atoms in the universe shifted. Other choices were not made. Other connections were not made. Other stories would never be told.

What were those stories? Other families? Different children? Different cities visited? A thousand other tales would never be told because this one would be told. This was the life story that was going to play out for them both.

One day at a time a life unfolds.

He finds that fascinating. You make one choice and a thousand other potential choices are erased. Life choices are so often made that casually until years later you reflect on what was missed . . . or not. Maybe you reflect on what you finally discovered and uncovered about yourself. The mystery reveals itself. In this case, it is happening on the day he dies. How ironic.

His mind races over the years. The first date. The first kiss. The first embrace. Ever think about the firsts of things? They only happen that once. The first time. There is a chill or shiver that goes up the spine on the first of things. It is the most exquisite of emotions . . . the first . . . and then gone forever. Ever wonder why we don't treasure them more? Given there is only one *first*.

Their first date was a movie and a few drinks at a quiet bar. There was a guitar player strumming romantic songs and singing softly in the background. Johnny Mathis was big at that time and was perfect for quiet first-date evenings.

He remembers the songs so vividly. "The Sweetheart Tree," "Chances Are," and "The Twelfth of Never" were just a few. The songs and the tavern mood set the stage for slow dancing on the small, postage-stamp-sized dance floor with fingers touching and caressing.

The first kiss was at a stoplight on the drive back to her home. The first embrace was at her front door when they were kissing good night.

A smile seems to appear on his face. But the nurse is no longer in the room and everyone else has stepped outside to discuss the grave state of affairs. No one is present to witness it.

Firsts and lasts have so much in common. It may not seem that way at first blush, but they do.

The lasts. The last moment in a life.

The last touching and caressing of fingers. The last slow dance. The last look into the eyes of someone who went the distance with you.

Where do you find yourself at the last?

He is in the intensive care unit. So maybe he needs to consider the moment before the last one. Where was it exactly–the next-to-last moment?

He hears her voice through the mist and fog of his mind. Is it her voice now or from years ago? Time is no longer linear. Everything seems to be a massive abstract painting without straight lines. Time and space are fluid. Everything is accessible as if it is all present whether past or not. It is all past present and present past. History was current events.

And so, when he hears her voice he needs to think what the topic is or was. Who was she talking about or with, and where was he at that moment? She told him that the kids needed help with their homework. Could he break away from the TV show and help them?

OK. It was the early '80s. Their daughters were in first and third grade. They were so sweetly trying to figure out elementary school! Why was he watching TV? Why wasn't he involved in their lives? That haunts him. Then? Now? Always?

He thinks about his children. One is all grown up now. One. One. That number, that word is stuck in his mind. She is married. She has a husband. She has two children. He has always been amazed that his baby had babies. He is a grandfather! The thought has always stopped him in his tracks. Two beautiful, little grandchildren. One of each, a boy and a girl. He loves them dearly and has enjoyed firsts again with them.

But their little one is gone. Their baby is no longer there. No longer growing up. How could that be? That loss changed everything. That death killed so much of who and what they were.

The word *courage* again flashes through his mind. *Put the pieces back together before it all ends,* was now echoing in his mind.

He was just turning the TV off to help with their homework. Why is it you don't appreciate what you have until it is gone? Gone. Is there a way to appreciate life in real time? Maybe there isn't. Life comes at you so fast and furiously. Bills, obligations, job, debts, distractions—with no true appreciation of time and the fleeting nature of it all. So, you live each day as if there are no consequences . . . but there are. *But then again,* he thought? . . .

If he had another chance would he/could he have taken it? Maybe we are always locked into the story no matter what. Or not. Who can say because . . . well, there is the rub. There is no second chance. He had thought he could learn from his mistakes, gain wisdom from failure, but there were no second chances. That is the problem with a life. There is just the first and last time and no do-overs. And when you get lost, as so many do, and as he did, first and last are one and the same.

The first and the last are unique. Ones of a kind. The main difference is that you don't know when the last will be, so you really can't plan for it. It kind of just happens. Many times, the last sneaks up on you without warning. Like this just happened. And exactly what did happen?

The nurse returns to the room. Everyone else enters the room again too. He hears whispering. He also hears himself say that he is sorry. He can't tell if he has actually said it or just thought it and is recalling a long-ago conversation.

She asks, "Sorry about what?"

He says, "Everything."

She asks, "What about everything?"

His memory takes him back to so many moments that called for a "sorry." Missed dinners and parties, thoughtless comments or gestures made as he was trying to solve a business dispute. None was as important as just being present with those who mattered. And some were just selfish moments. Moments of self-absorption.

Self-absorption.

"What I want trumps what anyone else wants" type thoughts.

And sometimes you simply get lost in the world with all its distractions. There are so many distractions. Once lost, you try to find your way back to yourself and to home. But many are not that lucky and never find themselves again. So many relationships are destroyed this way. If you are lucky, you maneuver the obstacles and detours.

He stops himself. He thinks, *We are all cracked cups. We are all flawed. Why can't we see the bruises on each other? In ourselves.* His mind then goes quiet.

The death chill comes over him.

As the body starts to shut down, its temperature begins to fall. Ever so slowly but falling nevertheless.

He feels his muscles getting stiffer and almost hardening. He feels cold. He must have shivered because someone puts a second warm blanket over him. It isn't going to matter but he thinks it is a nice gesture. Nice gesture. He is going to miss nice gestures. A simple thank you. A kind touch when you feel alone even in a crowd.

She walks out of the room. She is exhausted. She doesn't want to say goodbye just yet, but that is where she has found herself. She knows there are merely a few moments left.

What was it about him she loved? In the early years, he made it difficult to love him. It was almost as if he was testing her love. He wasn't. She saw something in him. Something clever, funny, irreverent, smart, and kind even when he exhibited none of those qualities. She still saw them in him.

They were so young back then. Neither knew what they were doing or what they were in for. But does anyone? We make choices. There are consequences. And so life goes.

He wonders if there is a god. He figures he will find out in short order, but he wonders just the same. And if there is a god, has HE or SHE stuck around after the creation to continue to participate in our lives or has God left the building, as Elvis used to do after his concerts ended? God. We need that belief, don't we. Or maybe not.

He wonders, *What does it all mean if there is no overarching plan? But what plan? Is all this just someone else's dream?*

Did he live his life in a way that he was "good" with meeting God or not? Was he a few breaths away from judgment? Judgment Day! What a concept. Why do we need that? A day of reckoning. Well real or not, he is approaching it. Again, he thinks, *Have courage.*

Although his eyes are closed, he thinks he can make out some things in the room. The room seems to be getting larger. In fact, it has fluctuated in size. Big. Small. Square. Round. At one point, flat. He even has felt himself hovering over the room a few times.

They decided to get married. Looking back on it, they were way too young. Why didn't their parents stop them? After marriage, they moved to Miami. From New York to Miami. It seemed like a good idea at the time. Are most decisions like that? Just seeming like a good idea at the time? A whole life not lived in one place to begin in another.

People you will never meet. Experiences you will never have. People you will meet. Experiences you will have. If you reflect on it, it could drive you crazy. Everything takes on geometric proportions. The friends of the people you meet or do not meet. It just goes on and on. Job opportunities, neighborhoods, community groups, schools, and every other type of connection or relationship becomes part of your life story . . . or not.

The entire fabric of life changes with a single choice.

He feels colder. He knows he is fading. His heartbeat is getting slower. There are longer pauses between beats. His pulses are getting further and further apart. He is becoming more confused. It must be the little oxygen circulating and barely making its way to his brain. Again, he shivers. This time there is no additional blanket. He figures that everyone knows it doesn't matter anymore.

Where was he? Oh yes . . .

They moved to Miami. It was still the early years there before the over construction started. Miami then still felt like a unique tropical setting. Unlike today where it feels like just another over-built city . . . just hotter all year round.

He got a job at a small law firm. That's right . . . he was an attorney. How did that happen? He wanted to be a teacher. Actually, a professor of history. He loved history. How one choice changed the lives of nations and many times the world always fascinated him. History was not about dates to him. It was about people, human frailty, decisions, and lives affected. Who was president or the leader of some other nation at a particular point in time and how those personalities could change the world and the lives of the citizens in each nation was fascinating. Wars. Peace. Genocide. Rescue. Liberation. Torture. How people got caught up in it or not. It all fascinated him. But he never got to write about or teach history because . . .

He was offered the opportunity to accept an assistantship at a fine college, but his dad, a survivor of the Great Depression, persuaded him to go to law school instead. Right? Wrong? He will never know because you can't live parallel lives. He always felt he would have been a great teacher, but maybe not.

He gives a slight cough. His body continues its path of shutting down.

He became a lawyer—a trial lawyer. So far from history classes. He would have studied modern history. Probably the foundation of the United States and modern Europe, Asia, and Africa, and how the people of these continents interrelated. His classes would have delved into how one nation's decisions affected other nations and the choices they made.

He would have written books and taught students to appreciate the past and see how it affects the present and could shape the future. But a lawyer he became. It was fine. He did well. Made a good name for himself, but there was a hole. The law became so mercantile. Realization rates. Billable hours. One big number-crunching machine.

He wonders how it all got so mercantile. It didn't start out that way . . . or did it? When did money, wealth, stuff take hold of everyone? How many lives did it ruin? The chasing after stuff. It became a national obsession. It made some people crazy or at least act crazy.

Wait . . . hold on. He thinks he hears something. More voices. More scurrying by people. Is something happening? To him? His mind wanders away from him again. He is traveling back in time again.

It was a conversation with his dad that changed his career path. It was that one moment. His dad's fear of a repeat of the Great Depression reached out from 1929 to touch his life over thirty-five years later.

Fear.

What a controlling emotion. It is probably one of the most powerful emotions that exist. He wonders how it controlled and shaped his life and the decisions he made. His dad's fear of not putting food on the table because his boss could fire him for any reason at any time was presented to him as a critical reason for choosing a career.

Fear of failure, he figures, made a lot of people do things they wouldn't ordinarily do or change the path of their lives. Interesting, he thinks, since the choice is made based on a perceived threat that may not even be real or ever happen, yet you give up a dream or move away from a chance to fulfill a dream, founded on something as abstract as an emotion that often freezes you in place.

So, was it entirely his dad's fear of his son reliving the Depression that sent him to law school? He remembers how much he disliked law school.

It changed him. It made him more cynical and argumentative with everyone and about everything. He changed. He doesn't think he changed for the better. Everything became a dispute to be won. Being clever and manipulating others were the keys to the kingdom. They didn't teach humanities in law school. Or morality. A little ethics.

Would it have been different in the history path he bypassed? He wonders. He has heard that college careers are pressure cookers too. *Publish or perish* was the catchphrase in "professorland."

But then again, the world changed so much during this period of time—these few decades. History seemed romantic to him. The context of events. Choices made. Good guys and bad guys. Maybe it was too simple. Beside romance seems to have died in the age of easy hookups and online everything. He always felt like a bit of an anachronism . . . someone who belongs in another time. A knight in rusty armor who . . .

His temperature drops again. He feels odd. Like his organs are no longer responding to the slightest normal type of function.

How did he get into fear? *How absurd,* he thinks. He is dying. Fear is no longer in the equation. It doesn't matter. Fear. Joy. Happiness. Sadness. Meaningless now. Yet emotions controlled so much during all the years of choices.

He feels her hand on his cheek. She whispers something. He thinks he hears the words, "It's okay."

What's okay? he thinks. Her.

She was always there. How did that happen? At this moment in time he is living his . . . their . . . life backward while she is still living it forward. Would they meet in the middle somewhere in time and reconnect on some holiday or romantic interlude before the final goodbye?

Her. There was always . . . her.

But what about her? How did that come to pass? How do two people decide to write a history together? He thinks that maybe you don't think of it that way. Maybe the mind can't fully comprehend the abstract concept of being with someone else on a journey for twenty or thirty . . . or forty or fifty or more . . . years.

He thinks that the glue that keeps people together might come down to feeling safe.

Safe.

That word never crossed his mind before when he thought about marriage and relationships. So much talk about getting married is about sex or lust or some physical attraction, but maybe it is all about feeling safe. Is safety the antidote to fear? But maybe that is what keeps people together. A need, a desire, for safety.

A tear runs down his cheek as he thinks about safety. He hears her say, "Look, is he crying?" She takes a tissue and begins to wipe it away then stops. It is as if she wants him to have all the last emotions she thinks he would want.

She has no idea what he is going through. How could she? How can anyone really know what another is going through? We have a hard-enough time knowing what we are going through, let alone someone else.

So here he is, traveling backward in time. *Is that the final journey?* he wonders. *The past becomes your present?* If that is the case, then he might as well relax and enjoy this final ride. Is this where death and birth connect? Is this the final solving of the eternal mystery? If that is the case, then maybe time will soon become irrelevant. Maybe a second or an hour or a day are the same. Could there be no difference? Maybe this is where relativity plays out its last sleight of hand.

His mind shoots back to high school. What a strange time for kids. You are really in between. Everything seems so personal and important. Everything seems so explosive on a minute-by-minute basis. You live in the present even as you are constantly thinking about and worried about the future. And oh, the peer pressure to conform to your little group of friends! You are told or lectured how each decision could affect and change the trajectory of your life! The pressure is always there, and this seems to be where comparisons really take hold. Comparisons are made to friends, other families, school jocks, creative ones, and the "different ones." The ones who want to be someone else.

When he was growing up, it was unclear. Gay, straight, trans were topics never discussed, or if they were, it was with confusion and nervous laughter. It wasn't meant in a nasty way, it was just a confused way of seeing something that was not your typical *Father Knows Best* episode. Back then certain things were just not talked about.

High school.

He remembers the first slow dance. The first make-out sessions. What was it . . . ? Oh yes, the game Seven Minutes in Heaven. That's what they called it. It seems so innocent in retrospect, but back then it felt so daring! He remembers not really knowing how far to go or when it was too far.

Back then it was all baseball when dating a girl. First base was touching with the clothes on, second base was . . . He is so weary. Third base was more intimate, and then the home run. From above the clothes touching to unbuttoning to . . . well, the batter either gets a base hit or makes a home run.

He doesn't think those distinctions would even be understood now. It seems so quaint now. The innocence of exploration of sex.

A fog is coming over his thoughts. He is so confused. Where is he now? He was home. Which home? What was he hearing? His mom and dad were fighting. Yelling. Screaming.

He hears something break. He twitches. That twitch sets the ICU in motion. He hears someone say that it is getting close. *Close to what?*

How did he get here? He was fine yesterday or a few yesterdays ago . . . wasn't he? What is yesterday anyway?

Her. His mind is on her again. She was safe. She was safety. She was better. Better than what? Better than him.

She was smart. Both book smart and human-being smart . . . you know IQ and EQ.

His memory takes him back to the connection between them. Why did she stay? Why didn't she just buck and run?

What happened on that one day? It was cold. Where were they? He is getting more and more confused. It is as if a thick cloud is descending over his brain. It is the type of fog that gets into everything. Filling every crevice.

He shakes his head trying to clear his mind. Everyone in the room jumps.

Secrets.

That word spontaneously appears before him. Secrets. There are so many. We all keep them. Sometimes we even trade in secrets. We use them as barter. Secrets. They can fill up a life. What is the toll they take?

A secret is something we don't want anyone else to know. Sometimes we just want to forget them ourselves even after we created them with our conduct or our words. The hidden part of a life. A crime never uncovered? A lie never revealed? A dishonest argument or transaction never made right? Every day in every way, they take place.

What is the effect on yourself and others? He once read a book titled *Hour of the Wolf*. The wolf prowling, haunting the night hours. Does the wolf get its strength from the effect of lies on a life?

His mind shoots back to her. She didn't keep secrets. She was an open book. She was transparent. Is that how they survived all the years? She was the looking glass? She was the conscience for both of them? Maybe that was it.

He feels a pain shoot through his left side. He winces. Something is going on inside him. What organ is slowly shutting down that is having a ripple effect on everything else inside him? He is dying before his very senses.

What a waste! That thought bounces around his head. How much time we waste. *Waste doing what?* Usually worrying about things that never did or even will happen. We are odd creatures, aren't we?

His mind takes him further back. He is on a swing. He couldn't have been more than six or seven. His dad was pushing him. He yelled to go higher and faster. He was laughing. So was his dad. Hearing his dad laugh was always a joy to him. His dad didn't laugh that often. It wasn't that his dad was sullen, it was just that his dad always seemed to have the weight of the world on his shoulders. His dad was a blue-collar worker but not a blue-collar type guy. His dad was more college professor in a working man's uniform of mud-brown color shirt and pants with the company logo on the front shirt pocket. But inside his dad was a teacher.

Maybe that is where he got his love of teaching from. A blue-collar college professor? The conversations between them . . . even then . . . focused on the mystery of life. The why. The how come. The what if. All throughout his life, he wondered about the why. Again, the same group of words splashed into his mind . . . *the how come . . . the what if.*

One conversation they had was about whether all life was just taking place in an evaporating drop of rain.

That always intrigued him. Just one drop of rain. Maybe there were millions of parallel universes playing out in millions of drops of rain.

His is evaporating now. He is transforming from solid to liquid to air. He is slowly going back up into the mist from where he came.

Being pushed by his dad on that swing is what fills his mind now. Oh, to relive that singular moment! It is simple moments like that have lingered in him.

Maybe the how come of life was time spent together. Was it that simple?

She is sitting in the ICU, long past crying. She is all cried out. Did they say what had to be said? Did they forgive each other? Did she say that she understood and loved him despite his imperfections? She knew she had her own imperfections and the two, together, caused many an issue and heartache over the years. And yet, they agreed to fight through the hurt and pain and disappointments. After all, she realized that marriage was complicated.

Marriage is confusing and has its mountains and valleys, but each couple makes a choice. Each couple decides to fight through the issues or give up. They had decided a long time ago to give each other a break from the condition of being a flawed human and to fight for their marriage to endure. They understood that it was easier to see the cracks in the armor of someone else than to study them in your reflection in the mirror. It is easier to be a critic than to be on a personal self-improvement course. They chose to go the personal self-improvement route and find the humor and decency in each other again, as well as to find the joy in the journey. There is both joy and sorrow. Yet, you have to embrace it all.

She thinks about the night he proposed. They were so young and naive. *Naive* being the big word. He asked his mom for the ring that his great-grandmother had left. It was truly an antique. Not her style yet quite the showpiece. He had it wrapped inside a rose and as she smelled the flower she saw the wrapping and opened it up to find the ring. He asked her to be his wife.

Considering they were both "babies" it was comical and sweet. Little did they know the laughter, tears, surgeries, heartache, births, and deaths that would consume them.

The death of one's child is an earth-shattering moment. It is unimaginable. It is the ultimate nightmare. It is the one thing no one wants to hear.

Her face gets flushed. Her mouth goes dry. She still has to shake her head in disbelief. It is a bad dream that she can't wake from. She thinks about how seconds matter. Those seconds change everything. And it was avoidable. She is shaking now. There are some pains that run so deep that the ache never stops.

Paradise. Does it exist? The Garden of Eden. Is it real? If paradise exists, does that mean that hell exists too? Is it a place or a state of mind? Is it an attitude about life? Is it an attitude about death? Is death the end or is there another chapter after the death chapter? Dust to dust? Or birth to rebirth?

Would he see their little girl soon or never again?

His body is becoming quieter. As his body moves toward its concluding page, will he have a chance to realize more . . . as he becomes less?

Was their little girl in Paradise? He told her he would see her there when she closed her eyes for the last time. Would he?

The last time . . . there it is again.

The first and the last of things. He had read in some book that your last thought is what you carry with you after you die. Carry to where he didn't know. But he wanted his baby's last thought to be sweet. He wanted her to carry sweetness with her wherever she was going. That idea had comforted him.

Could he focus his mind on sweetness as his last thought or would it be darker than that? He doesn't want his last thought to be about secrets. Or sadness. Or regrets. Or hate. Or loss. Or his negligence. Or his self-absorption. He wants it to be about something kind and good and decent. Something bright and glowing with gentle thoughts.

If he is to carry the last thought forward into death like some necklace or chain, he wants it to be light, airy, joyful, and filled with hope. Maybe he has to come to terms with the events in his life that led him to act so carelessly before he can be open to the straight path to the paradise he hopes existed for all frail beings like him.

She is tired. She wants to leave the hospital but feels sure that if she does she will get the call that he has died at the very moment she steps out. She is, after all, the "adult" in the family. The responsible one. She hates being the responsible one but no one else seems prepared to pick up that mantle.

She pulls up one of the metal chairs in the room and sits in it. She stares at her husband. Forty years. It seems ridiculous, but they have just celebrated forty years of togetherness. Well, not togetherness. Married forty years. Together forty-seven, between dating, engagement and the marriage. She doesn't factor in the times they were separated. Ultimately, they decided to fight through those times and not give up on a history that told quite a story of love and commitment. They were good people with flaws, and flawed people who exhibited all the good judgment and bad judgment of everyone who has ever spent more than a week (or maybe even a day) trying to navigate life with someone else by their side.

He seems smaller in the hospital bed. He has withered even over the last few hours. His hair is matted down with sweat. His cheeks are hollower. She remembers both her mother and his mother's looks just before they passed. He has the same look.

PAUL R. LIPTON

His lips have become more pronounced. His teeth seem to fill up his mouth as the cheeks sink deeper into his face. It is the death mask. The death face.

She thinks about her mom. Then about his. Women of a different generation. Housewives forced by time and circumstances to go out into the business world. They really wanted to be home, taking care of the family.

She remembers taking home ed classes in high school. Really? Seems crazy now. She became the matriarch of the family after their moms died. Her dad and his dad died way before their moms did. She really is the elder in the family. The previous generation of elders was gone in their family. She became the elder one. She doesn't want to be but it seems like no one else stepped up to do the work that had to be done as a patriarch or matriarch.

She thinks about how her husband worried so. There was always something to take up the oxygen by worry. She found it exhausting over the years but his odd sense of humor and inherent decency, even when he acted dumb, kept her by his side. *Funny,* she thinks. *I raised him and, in the end, after the terrible twos and rebellious teen years, he turned out just fine. Better than fine.* Their marriage had settled into an easy rhythm.

The death of their daughter was always there, between them, and it haunted them but . . . and this was the big but . . . they each reconciled themselves to it in their own unique ways.

In the beginning, there was incredible grief. In the beginning, there was unbelievable regret and guilt. At

* 32 *

the outset, there was anger beyond description and a tearing at each other. It was more than tearing. It was a ripping and trying to shred the other. They didn't know what else to do. But then it was as if a light broke through the tears and cuts and bruises. It was as if GOD stepped in and shook them both.

They realized that no one gets out of life alive. We are born and in that instant of birth begins the dying process. All the mortality tables give reasonable lengths of time before natural death. But this was not a natural death. They began to understand that either a person travels to death or death meets up with a person on death's terms.

They began to accept that death comes to us all, so it is not the length of a life that matters but the quality, the touching of a soul that matters—and this can happen in an instant.

Still they missed her. They missed her laugh. Really a giggle. The sparkle in her eyes. Those cheeks . . .

The nurse comes in and breaks the spell. Some bell has gone off at the nurse's station. She didn't hear it since she was so deep in memory.

What happened? It was the pain drip that had run out. He is slowly twisting on the bed. He is dying and in pain now too. Maybe it is the stitches, a cast, or broken bones, or just the organs shutting down and stopping whatever is still barely functioning.

His mind is now in spring . . .

It was springtime. It had to be in the late '90s. Maybe '96? Or '97? Where were they? Not the Himalayas. That was earlier. Not the Matterhorn. That was a few years after the trip to Nepal. It was Normandy, France. His mind races around the scene.

They were at a small chateau. In the countryside. They had just gotten back from visiting Omaha Beach. They were sitting in their room. There was a balcony. It overlooked the village. Where was it? Close to Mont Saint Michel? Why did this pop into his head? What did he have to revisit there?

Oh yes.

Sacrifice. And courage again. What concepts.

Sacrifice and courage are not talked about these days so much in the age of selfies and social media surface conversations. You know . . . the latest this or that. But there was a time, not that long ago, when sacrifice and courage had a place in the world. In fact, a place of honor.

The giving of yourself for a bigger cause or another person. Seems almost alien now. A truly foreign thought. Sacrifice even seems a little stale now, an old-fashioned romantic notion. He thinks that the world could use the ideals of sacrifice and courage more than ever now.

But World War Two was a time of ultimate sacrifice. Today it is hard to think about people voluntarily making the ultimate sacrifice. He thought she would.

But he wasn't certain about himself. He always said he would for his family, but it never came up.

Then again, after their little girl was gone, he remembers asking GOD if he could trade places with her. He would gladly give anything to trade places with her, but this idea was mere fantasy. It was all after the fact.

What compels one person to give his life for another?

A sacrifice usually means giving up something for another thing that is considered of greater importance or significance. Sacrifices seemed to be everywhere remembered in Normandy. Especially at the cemetery, you could hear the whispers of the dead. The breeze carried their calling . . . *"Remember courage . . . Remember what is really important . . . Please remember me."*

He remembers walking by and through the rows of gravestones. So many marked "unknown." He thinks about that. They made the ultimate sacrifice and they weren't even "known."

Would someone trade places with him now as he lies in this hospital bed? There are no offers. But he doesn't think he would be a taker of any offer anyhow under these circumstances. He realizes it is his time. He has played out his hand and it is now time to throw the cards into the pile and call it a life.

Was there something more to be done?

There is always more to be done but time doesn't care. Time is arbitrary. Time is too cold and unfeeling. Bizarre when you think about it. Feeling, emotional people traveling in the medium of time that is unfeeling, cold, unforgiving, and could care less about any one story or any story for that matter.

Time.

That is the next thought that appears to him. He remembers reading *Einstein's Dreams*. What a clever, witty, compelling book. In it, time was discussed in so many different ways. One way was the ability to travel to the center of time. The center of any unfolding event. Freeze it and study it.

He thinks again about his little girl. Maybe this is to be his final journey through time. Travel back to that moment, freeze it in his mind, and finally better understand it before everything goes to black. Maybe that is why he is still lingering here. Maybe that is why he has to stay. He feels he has to understand and let others know the why, the how come, the explanation of the unexplainable.

His mind goes blank for a moment. It seems like so much time has passed, but he begins to think everything is really all happening inside a few seconds. Doesn't life always happen in seconds? Who invented the clock and calendar anyway? Who says a day is a day? A day could just as easily be a millisecond as twenty-four hours.

He lets his breath out.

The first of the five breaths is gone.

There are just four left. Can he figure the mystery out in these last four breaths? Four breaths. Normally so few are ignored. But now they are the time needed to solve the final mystery that has haunted both him and her for the last thirty years. This mystery has always been the unspoken thought that overlaid every waking moment. Every conversation. Every laugh and every tear. It was their haunting. The ghost thought that was just always there.

He needed to get here. He now wills time to slow even more. He pleads. He begs. Who will answer this prayer? He has to push on.

Breath Four

We are never prepared for some moments, even if you know they are a possibility.

He has always remembered the day. It never faded. Never got stale. It is one of those moments that is forever frozen in time and place.

Although the day started out sweet, it crumbled when they had an epic argument. About? The usual. Work getting in the way of family. The constant strain of clients pulling him away and the feeble excuse of "How do you think we would have all this stuff if I don't respond to the clients?" It was Sunday, a bright summer day. They were at the beach house. It was the place they went to try to escape arguments but didn't. Life follows you wherever you go it seems.

The beach house. Sanibel Island. A spot plucked out of time. No traffic lights. A few stop signs. One main road . . . Periwinkle . . . and one secondary road that went past Casa Ybel Resort. They usually drove over on Friday afternoon and back to Miami either Sunday night or Monday morning. They'd bought the house only a few years before. It was an isolated house on a side street, hidden behind trees. A fun house initially, this was a place where you could escape the routine and pretend you were lost on a deserted island in the middle of the Gulf of Mexico. You could hear Jimmy Buffet everywhere. She remembered that he liked: "If the phone doesn't ring, it's me." That song fit right into the Sanibel rhythm. In fact, there was no phone in that house.

The house was a place where there was no need for phones. It was wine, cheese, long walks, quiet beach days, and riding the bicycles past the local restaurants and small shops. Except for a pharmacy, a hardware store, and a Dairy Queen, there were no chain stores on the island.

Usually, they got up late, had breakfast, took the bikes out to the beach and then figured out lunch and dinner as the day unfolded. The kids loved it. It was family time and they got the attention they needed and often didn't get during the week. Basically, he tried hard to be present. She tried hard to be interested in his latest legal case.

It was a late Saturday afternoon. His mind surveyed the moment. He had talked for a month or so about fixing the screen door that opened to the upstairs deck. She was tired of nagging him, so she stopped. Why didn't she just hire a handyman like every other time something broke?! Like so many other things, the screen door was always discussed but not fixed. It was constantly on the to-do list and never done.

The upper outside deck had recently been redone by a handyman. New wood slats and a railing were installed. The project was just finished a few weeks earlier. The handyman was not the most efficient or careful in his work, but the price was right. Everything on the island tended to be overpriced, and this particular worker's fee was more reasonable. Since they weren't there during the workweek, they had to rely on the quality work of the various tradesmen who did jobs for them around the house. It was easy to accept everything without too close an inspection or argument.

Choices like this are made all the time. They seem no big deal at the time, but then the results of the poor choices often come back to haunt us.

By the time the handyman was nailing the last section of the railing in place he had realized he'd miscalculated the cost of the job and way underbid it. He was now pretty much working for nothing, and he wanted to end this job that day and move on to his next. He was finishing his third beer of the afternoon while listening to one last replay of Jimmy Buffet's "It's Five O'clock Somewhere" and "Cheeseburger in Paradise" and hammering the last few nails in place. There should have been four nails. Each nail should have been two inches in length. But he only had one nail left in his toolkit and the nail was only one inch in length. On top of that, he did not drive the nail in straight.

And so, the tragic stage was set.

He twists in the hospital bed. He gives out a moan. Everyone in the room draws closer, figuring that this is the final moment. The last dying gasp. But they don't know he is back there. Reliving the moment of loss. The pain. The guilt. The heartache. The death of a sweet child. The downward spiral of their other sweet daughter. The death of hope. Of love. Of decency. Almost the loss of a marriage and of both his and her sanity.

He had to stop himself. He didn't want his last thought to be reliving the pain. Is that what he would take with him to the other side? He forced himself to go back further to the weekend before that weekend.

What were they doing? Kayaking. All of them. It was so much fun. Kayaking through the mangroves off the coast of Sanibel. Getting stuck in the shallow water. He got out and had to pull the kayak through the murky water, feeling anxious about snakes and alligators, then hopping back into the kayak with everyone laughing. Family time. Precious innocence. Love.

After they finished the mangrove visit they got on the bicycles with child seats on the back and went over to the farmers' market. They splurged, buying frozen ice pops, popcorn, and cotton candy. A rare, if ever, treat that, for some reason, on this day seemed right. They laughed and chased each other from booth to booth and then went over to Jerry's Foods to pick up dinner. Salads, chicken, coleslaw, and cupcakes rounded out the shopping. The dinner was a true family affair. Laughter and feeling blessed to be together. They didn't know what was ahead. How could they? None of us ever do.

He was now back to the day he wanted to forget and wished had never happened.

Looking down at him in the bed, she's thinking about the same day. She doesn't remember the day well. But some details are still clear to her. For instance, it was overcast and there was a chill in the air. They had decided to stay in most of the day and do their own things, so to speak. He was upstairs reading the Saturday paper. She was downstairs cleaning up and putting the dishes away. They would be heading back over to Miami on Sunday morning this week because he'd told her that he had to get ready for a big hearing in court that Monday.

The kids were playing hide and seek. Going from room to room, they looked for and easily found each other. So, the fun of the hide-and-seek balloon was deflating. The little one decided to hide on the outside deck. When her sister's eyes were closed, she ran through the living room and grabbed the screen door. Her sister yelled, "Ready or not here I come." When she heard that, she giggled and bolted out the screen door, which gave way too easily because he'd forgotten to fix it. The spring in the door was not there. It just flew open and she fell through it, running fast. Her momentum propelled her directly toward the railing with its sole one-inch-long, crooked nail railing.

He heard the crack. He sensed something was going terribly wrong. He felt his world crashing. A flood of nausea hit him. He heard the scream. He heard, "Help Mommy." He heard the running through the house. He jumped up and ran down the stairs and through the house to the deck.

His wife raced out the front door and into the backyard.

He froze. Then he looked over the railing. His wife had just made it to their little girl's body. She wailed as she grabbed their precious child who lay there in a contorted position, looking like a broken Raggedy Ann doll. He screamed. She said, "Call nine-one-one!"

The little one was still breathing but her breath was faint. They learned later that her neck broke when her body hit the ground. All he remembers now, in his death state, was a fog and flurry of actions, movements, lights swirling, sirens, and different voices shouting different medical terms.

It was all so avoidable. None of it had to happen! All he had to do was fix the damn door! All the handyman had to do was put the right nails in the right places— and use the right number of nails! Or all he had to do was take the family out that day. Or all he had to do was play with them. Or. Or. Or. His mind faded out.

Please let me forget. Please let me go to her now. Please forgive me. Please. Please. Please, he thinks.

She remembers it slightly differently. She was cleaning the house. She asked him to do some chores. Fixing the door was high on the list. It always flew open and it always clanged shut when they would swing it closed. It was annoying. "Please do me a favor and just run over to the hardware section at Bailey's General Store and pick up a new spring for the door," she'd said. It really would have taken no time at all, only requiring a screwdriver and a few screws. The whole thing from driving to and from the store to screwing in a few screws and putting the door in place would have taken a half hour . . . maybe less. But he was in his "It's the weekend and it is no big deal" mood, so it never got done.

She was cleaning because she wanted to get the angry energy out of her. She had planned to call a handyman then changed her mind because . . . because why? Because she wanted HIM to do it!

The kids were running around. She was in no mood for the noise! She whispered to her little one, "Go play and hide outside. Just go. Get out of my hair . . . dear!" And so, the little one did what her mom suggested. Only if. Only if. Only if. *Please forgive me. Please let me forget. Please. Please. Please,* she thinks.

The funeral was surreal. The casket was so small. They both looked down. They couldn't look at each other. Afterward, the clothes were packed away. The dolls and other toys were left in her room. It became a sort of toy memorial. A reminder of an angel. A reminder of the frailty of it all. A reminder of not realizing how fleeting it all is. A reminder of both the quantity and quality of a single life. A single second.

Consequences of choices. Results of decisions. Everything changed after their daughter died. A sadness fell over the entire family even at supposedly happy times. Really, there were no happy times anymore. There were just less painful times. It was just levels of pain. Some days were tolerable. Other times not even close. Yet, life must go on. Otherwise all would die with one death.

They still had their older sweet little girl. But she was never quite the same. She blamed herself. Why did she always find her sister's hiding places? Because she knew she cheated. She always kept one eye slightly open. Why did she have to win all the time? Why did she cheat? Why did she yell so loud that her baby sister ran faster to the screen door? *Why. Why. Why.*

The ripping of each other and themselves had continued for years. The tearing at themselves. The torment of a singular moment in time was always present.

The clock in the hospital room seems to be ticking louder. She looks at her husband and whispers, "I forgave and forgive you. Who knows why life plays out the way it plays out? Who can say? We can't carry the anger around forever. If you don't release it at the moment like this, when do you?"

She leans over his face. She studies it. She can tell the lines in his face that formed after that day. Deep lines. Exaggerated lines. Lines of grief. Lines of self-loathing.

He senses movement in the room. It isn't another person coming in. It isn't someone leaving. What is it? It feels good. It feels clean. What does this mean that it feels clean? *Pure.* Yes, a better word. It feels pure. Actually, it feels like a divine spirit has entered the room.

Is it God? Is it time?

He thinks he hears a voice. He recognizes it instantly. A tear runs down his cheek. Again, his wife decides not to wipe it away.

And then he hears the words he needs to hear. "Daddy, it is okay. Daddy, I am fine. Daddy, it is nice here. Daddy, can you see me yet?"

Deep inside he gives out a sigh. Deep inside he knows he is now living in a state of grace. Deep inside he knows he is about to receive the ultimate gift. The gift of forgiveness. But will it be enough?

The sorrow he felt has always consumed him. He has felt himself holding his breath. Now he tries to release the built-up guilt that had sapped him, her, and their marriage. He wants his wife to know their little girl is safe. That she is here with them. Is present in the room.

Her little hand touches his chest, which is covered by the hospital blanket. The blanket moves and there is a small indenture left where her little hand touched it. His wife sees the handprint on the blanket. She is confused by it, yet somehow knows something momentous is about to happen. She understands that at moments like this the potential is there to live in a state of grace. A state of salvation. That God exists. That God forgives. That what happened was human frailty that none of us can escape.

It was the human condition that caused the family to break and suffer but it is time . . . time to heal before the last breath. Without forgiveness, there is no humanity. Without forgiveness, there can be no salvation. And without salvation there is nothing.

She begins to sob. It is as if she is being released from the prison of being human. Being a parent. Being a flawed human being. She puts her hand on the small imprint she sees on the blanket. Her hand, the imprint, his chest.

She then takes her daughter's hand in hers and holds it on the blanket. Their daughter was such a light in their lives. But she too needed to find salvation. She too needed forgiveness. They all hold each other one last time. Maybe this is the very last time.

The tears rolled down each of their faces. They knew they are together again. It feels so good. So beautiful. So complete. So one. One. That is it: They are one again. A complete family. Whole. Beautiful. Loving. Kind.

They are all back in the living room. They are all so young. They are telling stories and laughing. He recalls that after dinner each evening they would gather in the living room and tell round robin stories. These were stories he would start and then point to another member of the family who would continue. At that point, the story usually twisted and turned in odd and funny ways. The story would go on until it ended with him saying . . . "The end." They would all laugh. They would hug each other. It was good.

As fast as this moment happened, that is as fast as it evaporated. His little angel is not there any longer. The spell is broken. He is just back in his hospital bed alone with his thoughts, which begin to wander again. This is out of his control. His mind feels like nothing more than a big movie screen that is playing disjointed segments of different movies about his life and the lives of those he loves the most.

He wants to go someplace else. He wants to be transported to another time and place.

He wonders what his life would have been like if just one thing was different. Any one thing. Big or small. He lets his mind run. *Would I be lying in this bed in this hospital? Would my death have been sooner? Later? Or does fate play out, in the end, the same way all the time?*

He remembers his dad telling him a story about death and fate. It was kind of biblical. His dad told him that

your date of death . . . not the how or why ,but the date
. . . was written in a big book of life held somewhere in
the sky. He thinks his dad said, "Heaven." A big book.
The book of life. His dad told him that since his dad
lived past the end of World War II, even though his dad
was not in the war, he would not have been killed in the
war because his dad lived past the war years. His dad
told him that it was written that way for all of us. Does
that mean that his little girl had been destined to die on
the day she did no matter where she was?

He wasn't certain if he felt comfort in that or not.
*The date is recorded in some book but the how and why
are left to chance?* Again, his mind goes racing.

There was one moment that could have changed it
all. It was the chance to live in France for a year. What
happened there? His mind cannot get focused on that
moment. Wait. It was . . . No, wait. He was twenty-two.

Was he ever really that young? College was drawing
to an end. Law school was approaching. But then the
call came in. His history professor called and asked if he
wanted to go to study in Paris. In particular, at the
University of Paris . . . now, Paris-Sorbonne. His
professor said there was a one-year course that he knew
would intrigue him.

Philosophy throughout time. The different "schools"
of philosophy. The different varied ways of living a life.
The meaning of time. Death. Hope. Destiny. God. The
devil. The social contract. And on and on.

He considered it but was thinking about law school
and "getting on with life." *What if?*

At that moment, it was as if a switch was flipped in his life. It was as if an exit ramp appeared and he took it. Not a detour but simply a new direction. Life is like that. No detours. Just a new destination and with that a different life story.

The Sorbonne is in the heart of Paris. He is there now. He has a small apartment in the Seventh Arrondissement. It is a walk-up. There is a cafe at the corner. He sits there for hours reading and reflecting. He learns basic French and immerses himself in the world of Paris. He attends classes and also walks the side streets and becomes friends with the shop owners. He loves the little shops. He becomes an expert in cheeses and wines. Three o'clock is his favorite time of the day. He sits with other students at different cafes drinking wine and eating the cheeses of the day with the best breads, rolls, and croissants that have ever existed . . . or so he believes.

It is glorious. It is there, between classes, wines, and loves that he starts writing his "opus." He tells his friends that it is about life in an age of uncertainty. How to live a life of purpose and self-determination in an age of profound uncertainty.

He had a working title for it: *Courage and the Uncertain Path.*

And there it is again . . . courage.

He concluded that as the world grows more technologically connected and there is a sense of control over our universe, in reality, we grow more uncertain of everything every day. We, in fact, lose control of our lives. We transfer our very existence, joy, and identity to a nameless, faceless entity . . . the air, the space between us, but not to or with each other. It is as if we are communicating in a vacuum of our own creation. Noise. Information, misinformation, nonfiction or fiction, illusion, floods the airwaves. We don't even know what is true anymore. It has become a world of opinions passing for facts. All of this floods the conversation. The noise overtakes the mind with crowded images that result in nothing more than uncertainty and confusion. Depression and mental health issues seemed to be expanding.

So, in his epic writing, he concludes that the object of life is to seek the personal definition, the personal code of honor, the personal moral compass, so that when you become flooded by uncertainty, which is everywhere, you can personally navigate the terrain of your life. He writes every day between classes and gatherings with friends. He writes into the late night and early morning.

He then starts studying the various religions and how each handles the trauma of uncertainty in the world. He discovers there is uncertainty even in the religions where supposedly there are clear answers and scriptures, like the Bible and other sacred texts—religions with quotes for every situation. He is curious to know how religions address uncertainty and chaos.

He keeps writing and reading and then finds his way to the Bhagavad Gita. It is this "song" that shifts his focus. It is that moment in which living each day fully and consciously intersects with the "law of uncertainty." He realizes that we each have to define ourselves clearly to and for ourselves. We have to be certain of who we were so that we can confront the uncertainty and built-in chaos of life. We have to be certain in our own purpose and personal mission so that the uncertainty of the world doesn't invade our core belief system.

He spends that year immersing himself in the essence of personal choice. But not untethered to the reality around him. It is just so clear to him that he needs to be unambiguous with who he is and what he believes.

At the end of the year, he has close to 300 pages of writing. He binds his manuscript together and puts a title on a cover sheet: *Courage and Personal Meaning in the Age of Uncertainty.*"

It is a little different title than the original thought but seems to say what he wants it to say.

He then puts a subtitle on it: *Living an Unambiguous Life.*

He makes a bunch of copies of it. He has typed it all with two fingers, a double-spaced manuscript written on a Remington typewriter. He mails one copy to his former history professor. He mails one to his Sorbonne advisor and one to the girl he hopes is still waiting for him back in the States. He mails a few more to some publishing houses but knows he is likely never to hear back. He is some unknown person writing about life, time, meaning, and purpose. There just are no readers for these concepts . . . or so the companies tell him in their rejection letters.

The writing itself has changed him. He is different. The girl is probably different too. But this journey had to be undertaken. A year in Paris. He doesn't know if he will ever come back.

An entire parallel life is taking place as he waits to die. Would he really be dying at this moment? His dad would have said yes. But who knows? Maybe he would be married to another woman, with other children, and living in some suburb of Paris. *Maybe my dad was wrong. Maybe I would have been some great philosopher known for creating the Courage in Uncertainty Institute,* he thinks.

The second world evaporates just as quickly as it appeared.

Decisions are made. The universe shifts and life then unfolds.

His body is shaking now. He hears the commotion in the hospital room. He is "back." His eyelids must have fluttered because he hears movement in the room by many people. Then it quiets down as he quiets down. He is calm now.

That road was not taken, but it felt so real. Uncertainty. Personal definitions. Didn't he talk about that in his life in a different context? He has often talked about finding your core principles and living a true-north life.

After all is said and done, we are still who we are no matter where we finally land.

She had asked her daughter to go home to care for her family. But their daughter had said that she was staying. It has been such a long day. The day has exhausted them all. Yet he is holding on. It feels as if each breath takes a lifetime. Each breath tells an important part of the ongoing story.

She thinks back to the way he used to sit at the computer in the evening. This actually was a fairly recent occurrence. He was writing as if possessed. He was muttering to himself about certainty in an uncertain world. It was as if he knew time was running out and he had to continue to write about overcoming chaos through personal choices.

He is thinking about the different lives we each could have lived.

He wonders if that is the way life is. Is that how life and death play out—in the end you live (or relive) the parallel paths you never took except on some alternate plane—or maybe in your dreams? Who can say.

PAUL R. LIPTON

It is so foggy to him now. What life did he, in fact, live? *This is nonsense,* he thinks. He knows the choices he made. She does too. The room becomes quiet again.

His mind begins to spin. It is clear to him that he is fading.

Fading. What an odd word to consider in thinking about a life.

Fading. It is normally defined as "becoming dim" or "losing the glow." Basically, "to gradually die." But then he remembers *fading* as being a term for some type of frequency interference in different radio waves traveling through time and space. Is that what he is experiencing, as his life is fading?

Are the alternate life choices, the parallel stories, fading into this life at the end? Is that how it all concludes? Reliving that which you never really lived but was a real possibility and desire? He thinks, *We are complex creatures.*

She sits down in the metal chair. Their daughter leans over the bed. His daughter wants to let him know that the life he shared with her has had meaning. That it was flawed, but she accepts that all of life is.

She remembers how she struggled after her sister's death. One of the biggest challenges her parents faced was getting help for her. She blamed herself. She went inside. She seemed to get smaller in size. She stopped eating for the longest time. She grew thin and pale. The laughter, the spark, the life in her eyes vanished. They were afraid that she would never be the same. Was her life to be haunted by the broken door, the broken railing, the broken hearts. She believed that her life was worthless . . . that the family was worthless. That the look in her parent's eyes would never be the same . . . especially when they looked at her.

It was not true, but she had felt helpless in her belief. As the years went by, she tried to get past that horrible moment, but it manifested itself in so many ways it was hard to escape it. She secretly began to cut herself. She cut herself in places she thought no one would see. Under her armpits. Behind her knees. Under her hair. But the cuts showed up in other ways. Her mood swings. Her highs and lows. Her nails that were bitten down to their nub.

One day she got a tattoo on her upper thigh. It was her sister's initials with a broken heart surrounding them. For some reason, it was this tattoo that started to turn her life around.

Her mom and dad tried to help. They tried to console her. But how do you get through to something that is this final? Somehow time began to heal the family. It may have been the trip they all took to a small monastery on Mount Baldy, California. That Zen center had been recommended to her father by a friend.

She shifts in the metal chair and closes her eyes. Grace comes in many forms. On that trip, it came to the whole family on a quiet, snowy morning.

They woke up early. Had a light breakfast and then went into the small sanctuary where the breakfast prayers were held. An elderly monk sat quietly with a few candles burning. The monk motioned for the family to sit on the small pillows that were placed before him. The three of them sat cross-legged on the pillows. He whispered a few prayers and then asked each to hold out their right arm. He then took a red string out of a white bag. He tied one red string around each wrist and said another prayer. He whispered that the red string was a symbol of protection, salvation, and a peaceful heart in a world that can be cruel and harsh.

The monk then turned to their daughter and said that she was released. That no one gets out of life unbruised and without struggles and that it is the quality and the good intentions of a person in each life that count. Life can be cruel and arbitrary and we each must continue to walk our path hopeful and to look up at a higher story of life and the afterlife. In life, it is the memories of laughter and joy that linger.

He then said something that changed all their lives going forward.

"Love survives death. And therefore, the love is always there with you. You kiss the ones gone and turn toward the new day, carrying the love forward. For both the ones left behind and the one that crosses over, love is the vehicle that transports you to your new tomorrow."

The monk said, "The red string will stay on your wrist for about a year before it falls off due to the wear and tear of the days. In that year, for all the time it encircles your wrist, touch it, feel it, stare at it, and know that you are safe, you are loved, you are forgiven, and you are loved by the ones left behind and the one who has moved on. Love is the salve that heals the broken heart."

She again shifts in the metal chair. She looks at her watch. It is so late. She stares at her husband. A man who struggled for forgiveness. She thinks she again is hearing him softly say, "Please, please, please."

She touches his hand. It feels colder now than just an hour ago. His skin seems a little bluer. The oxygen pulsing inside him is thin. The warmth that is his life is leaving him. The cold that is death is arriving. She leans down to his ear and simply says, "Yes, yes. Of course."

She is exhausted. She sits back in the chair and seems to nod off.

As she nods off, her mind travels back to Mount Baldy. She knows that a moment of grace saved their marriage. Probably it saved one or both of them from a life of despair, emptiness, and bitterness. And that sacred time saved their daughter. She is grateful. He was different after Mount Baldy.

A light seems to be rekindled in her. Her eyes seem clearer and more open to the life ahead of her.

He seems calmer, more complete, and no longer self-loathing. He seems to accept himself with all the blemishes life has added to his frail human frame.

Her mind drifts and takes her to the night they first made love. It was frightening and glorious. Intimacy was always a challenge for her.

Privacy. Private. Intimate. Totally your own. Belonging only to you, yet then you let someone else in . . . into your private universe.

She remembers from the time she was a little girl how she was taught that her "privates" were hers alone. "Don't let anyone else see 'it' or touch 'it,'" she was told in third grade by a lady who came to her class to talk about safe and unsafe touching. Unsafe touching always had something to do with her vagina or any part of her below her waist, and her chest and nipples. Being touched was always talked about as a taboo. "Don't play doctor or nurse with your friends" and "After a certain age stop bathing with your little friends that you used to bathe with" were rules she was to follow. It was confusing to her as she started to grow up.

When she got her period, she was terrified. No one had warned her about it. When she first started to bleed down there, she was ashamed. She did not know why but she was. Maybe it had to do with Adam and Eve and their banishment from the Garden of Eden. She wasn't certain, but she was scared. In time, she would learn and be told all about it—usually by her girlfriends, who always seemed more knowing about these things than she did.

Of course, then came junior high school and high school. Her first real date was frightening for her. In addition to her friends' chatter, she read books about forbidden romances from the olden days . . . *Romeo and Juliet* . . . and saw movies about teen romance and escapades. She didn't know what was acceptable for a "nice" girl to do. How far was too far? She would hear the boys laughing about first base, second base, third base, and a home run. She heard about French kissing and would look at herself in the mirror as she tried to imitate a French kiss. It looked silly and odd to her. She would talk to her friends about exchanging saliva with some guy. Again, it seemed strange to her. Then she wondered about what was acceptable for her to do with a boy. She heard about "boners" and "hard-ons" and wasn't certain what you were supposed to do with them. One of her friends who sounded more experienced explained her options on handling a guy's privates. She just listened and wondered.

It wasn't until she was around fifteen that she ventured into the intimacy arena. It was with a boy she had a crush on, and they went to a make-out party. The experience was awkward and sloppy. Thinking back on it now makes her laugh with bemusement. It was just so confusing to her. Hands were everywhere. His were trying to touch her in all the places she was told as a child were her privates and her hands were kind of touching his parts. They exchanged saliva, felt each other in all sorts of places, and then she heard him moan and felt wetness on the outside of his jeans. When that happened, he just stopped what he was doing and got up and went to the bathroom. She felt confused and a bit ashamed. She didn't know why she felt ashamed; she just did. She never went out with that boy again. Or more honestly, he never asked her out again.

Some friends told her that they heard from friends of friends that he thought she was nice but seemed too timid and unsure of herself. He had confided in a friend that she was a nice girl. He just didn't want a nice girl . . . yet.

After that, she had other dates and held back from touching. She wasn't very trusting of what would happen and why it would happen.

And then she met him.

He was different from the other boys and young men she went out with. By this time, she was guarded in what she would do and not do. She'd had some sexual experiences, but only light ventures into the area. But he was different. He seemed really interested in her as a person and not as just some conquest. He was very talkative, funny, and wanted to just be with her. Walking, holding hands, kissing her on her nose and forehead, as well as on her lips.

The night they first made love it seemed honest. It seemed natural. It seemed as if it came from a place of caring and tenderness and not someplace that was just body parts exchanging fluids. It seemed personal. She remembers that it was romantic. They made love to each other. Each taking turns in some adventure into the senses. She was relaxed in finally releasing her tensions and trusting that she was safe with him.

Safe.

The word ricochets through her mind. Maybe she needed to feel safe and secure, so she could be intimate. The lovemaking was just that. It seemed to be founded on loving and caring for the other. By the time they made love she felt love for him. She sensed that he loved her and loved being with her.

Love.

The antidote to fear of intimacy. They didn't have sex that night. They made love. There was a kindness to his loving her. A gentleness. An appreciation of the gift she was giving to him. It was sweet. She finally began to understand what all the fuss was about. There was desire mixed with compassion. Passion mixed with affection. This became their connecting tissue. This became their bond. They wanted to please each other. They wanted to bring pleasure to each other. It was unselfish.

And that is the way it was with them. Even through the tough stretches, when it came to intimacy, there was an understanding that something was happening between them and it was a moment of respect and appreciation of being open, caring, and passionate, with compassion balancing it all out.

She nodded to herself. This was the saving grace of their connection. The little girl opened up to the little boy and they relaxed into the moments of joint bliss.

She slips on the metal chair and is fully present in the hospital. She looks over at him . . . her little boy. She thinks again of that first moment of intimacy. She reaches for his hand. It is so cold. Looking down at him she wonders, *Where are you, my first love?*

He doesn't have any awareness of her touch. His dad's image has appeared before him.

His dad. The way his dad died was such a sad and confusing ending to a decent man's life. Life gets so complicated. Sometimes things happen that are not explainable even if the words keep pouring out.

It all happened in a New York minute. He always liked that phrase until it resembled another tragedy in his family.

A New York minute. Really an instant. Way less than a real minute. You know what it is . . . the time between when you order a coffee and when you asked if it is ready . . . already. He always used this phrase at work. "Be there in a New York minute."

But then, one day, it all changed. Sometimes you need time to reflect, consider the choices and the consequences of those choices. Some consequences are irreversible. Some choices are draconian. Sometimes a person gets so confused in life that the worst thing to do is to decide something in a New York minute. Yet, that is what happened. Not to him but to his dad.

He twitched in the hospital bed. But nobody saw. She was dozing in the metal chair and never saw the twitch. Not that it would matter.

It was a cold day in New York. He doesn't remember much about it. It was just a typical winter day in the Northeast. Maybe December? Could have been January. His dad was a salesman for a trucking company. The Miller-Sweet Hauling Company. It was a local hauling company that did jobs throughout the state. His dad went to different businesses to sell the hauling services.

This was not a job his dad wanted, liked, or was even suited for, but time took its toll on his dreams and that's how he paid the bills. His dad felt lost and lonely in the job. His dad always believed he was destined for a more exciting line of work, but the Great Depression had changed all that. He could just tell. His dad's job was not challenging enough, it was way below his skill set. Still he did it. Life didn't seem fair. Whenever he had looked at his dad, he always saw a Willie Loman type figure—like in the play *Death of a Salesman.* It wasn't a fair nor accurate portrait, but it seemed to fit his father's dissatisfaction, even if it fit like a cheap poorly tailored suit.

Willie was a tragic hero, honest, still believing in the American dream, but left behind by life. His dad seemed similar. Why his dad decided to leave work early that cold day and take the Long Island Railroad into Penn Station would never be understood. Why he walked down the street to the Chelsea Hotel and took the elevator to the top floor and went out on the roof was puzzling. Much later he learned that his dad sat there for hours in the freezing cold before he jumped!

The police called it a clear suicide. It was not an accident. His dad wasn't meeting anyone up there. The whys and how comes would never be fully known. There was no note or letter left anywhere, although he did take off his wristwatch and leave it in the roof ledge. Who knows why. Maybe he wanted someone to know the time he had left this earth. He had cracked the glass on the watch, so it was frozen in time. Or maybe it was just because it had been a gift from his wife. It was not an expensive watch, just a regular Timex, but clearly, he had wanted to leave something behind.

His mom later talked to him about the despair his dad felt with his life choices and the hand he had been dealt. He didn't completely appreciate those fine points at the time.

Why was this racing through his mind now? What was the impact his father's suicide had on his life and his choices? He had never talked about how his dad died to anyone. He would just tell people his dad had died when he was a younger man.

He told his own wife the story, but no one else. For the longest time, he was ashamed, and then he had just put it out of his mind. Until now. Now, in the few moments before his death he was remembering it again. Maybe this was understandable. Maybe it was the last, only way his dad could prove to himself that he controlled his destiny and he was not merely going to fade away as some pathetic afterthought of a life.

Fade. There is that word again. Do we all want to avoid fading away? Don't we want to make a statement about something before we exit stage left?

And so now, in his own moment of fading, he is commanding his mind to go back to understand better his journey. The journey we all take. The fate that awaits us as we vanish from this slim slice of time.

He reflects. Did his dad really finally control the end play by killing himself or was this just another example of a man being controlled by others, cruelly manipulated into this self-destructive turn of events? He recognizes that his dad's death affected his choices and attitudes.

For example, he was combative and pushed his agenda forward whether completely satisfied with it or not. He was louder than certain situations called for and dressed a bit too flashy. He wore bright colors and trendy fashions that were a little ahead of their time. As the years went by, he made choices to change jobs when he felt work was getting stale. He was always moving to another law firm to avoid being bored or becoming fully defined by others.

He wanted to be a bit of a mystery, and he succeeded. Some people thought he was aloof. Others thought him a bit shy. Some thought he was a little smug. But all thought he was very clever and smart. It was as if he knew the answer but wasn't going to share it until he was damn ready. He actually had thought he had some answers.

But now he understood the human paradox. Live, succeed, buy, sell, love, hate, win, lose . . . die. It's absurd. Death can do that to you. Death uncovers the absurdity of it all.

And so there he was. His dad's story began to evaporate into the ether. He regrets that he didn't have more time with him. He would have liked to have learned more from him, even if it was from a failed effort point of view. Maybe he would have adjusted his "style." Maybe he would have eased up on others and not moved around so much. Who knows? Who knows anything?

She wakes up from her short nap. She notices that he is a bit crooked on the bed. She adjusts his body. His breathing is shallow. She suddenly thinks about his dad for some reason. She hasn't thought of him in years. Odd.

As she stretches in the small metal chair, his mind focuses on his mom and how things unraveled for her after his dad died. Saying her life was *tragic* doesn't even come close to catching the events fairly.

He knew it all changed for everyone after his dad's death, but the most devastating change was to his mom. His parents had met when they were so young. His mom was much younger than his dad, but they were both still young. She was eighteen when they started dating and only nineteen when they got married. They met during the Second World War. Life was simpler back then. Not easy, just simpler. There was no TV or other distracting gadgets like that. There was the radio, newspapers, and magazines. The telephone was an oddity. Even he could recall shared "party lines" and the novelty of calling someone on the phone. That was normal for his folks' generation.

After they married, his mom and dad lived in small rental apartments in the Bronx, and later in rental houses in Queens. Eventually, they bought their first home on Long Island. The New York City suburbs were just being developed. A whole new world was being created right before their eyes. It was both exciting and frightening. They could sense that the world was changing and would never be the same.

All through those years, his mom was a housekeeper. His dad would go to work while she stayed home to clean, do laundry, shop for groceries, and plan their evening meals. Home Education was even being taught to girls in junior high schools and high schools. His mom went from teenager to housekeeper in the blink of an eye. She struggled with it. It seemed like unimportant work to her even though it became the backbone of an entire generation. Her generation of women would go on to redefine the home and child care in these post-World War Two years. But it did require everyone to adjust.

His dad was the "breadwinner," and his mom was the "home preserver." She maintained the "castle," albeit a small cookie-cutter home castle. After all, this was the Levittown years . . .. whole developments of single-family box-type houses. The years were the late 1940s and early 1950s when the demographics and migrations occurred from city to suburb. He thought that no one was really ready for it. But there she was . . . a homemaker.

She settled into the routine. Breakfast for her husband in the morning, then her second cup of coffee, dusting around the house, food shopping, chatting with neighbors . . . all new to his mom . . . cooking a balanced, healthy dinner and, once the kids came, raising them.

Her sons came in short order after they moved to their first house. Being left with the kids alone each day was challenging. At that time there was no daycare centers or other such services. So, it was her and the kids waiting all day for Daddy to come home.

Those were the years of a lot of waiting around and trying to find things to do all day. Scrapbooks, coin collection, stamp collections, finger painting, marbles (playing and trading them), coloring books, collecting baseball cards, and reading were big moments in an otherwise lazy day as he and his brother were growing up. There wasn't even new music.

It was all the parents' music. At least until Elvis arrived.

He tried to shift himself in the hospital bed. He did not want to lose this train of thought. He went back to it . . . where was he? Oh yes . . . with his mom after his dad's suicide.

His mom had no idea her husband was as despondent as he was. His mom knew he was dissatisfied and frustrated . . . but she was too. She had never dreamed that her life would become cooking and cleaning. She had wanted a career too, but those things weren't discussed. On the day his dad died, his mom was home reading and . . . she had taken up knitting . . . knitting a sweater as a gift to some friend.

The police came to the house and let her know the body had been found. It had been hours since he died but they brought the news in person. Back then life was more personal and less immediate than today. Back then, life involved more face-to-face communication. There was no texting, no email.

He really doesn't remember a lot more about the aftermath of his dad's demise other than the tears, the hysteria, the funeral, and the sense that something life-changing had happened to them all, but mostly to his mom. She was never the same.

His mom tried to put on a strong face, but she was fifty-three at a time when this was not the new thirty-three. It was more like . . . well . . .close to being a senior citizen, in that day. But she didn't feel that way. Senior. She still felt like she had something to do though she wasn't trained for anything other than being a wife, mom, and housekeeper.

Her options were narrow. His dad left nothing behind . . . no life insurance or savings of any kind. There was the house with a mortgage and that was it. There was a little social security. He sensed that his mom felt that she was just going to be alone in the remaining years of her life.

Both he and his brother felt helpless and were not too helpful in any way. They just weren't ready for all the things that started raining down on them.

And so, the stress, strain, loneliness, and sense of emptiness ate her alive. At night, the worst time of the day for her, she started drinking and taking sleeping pills. He knew something was wrong because in the mornings she slept late and was groggy and disoriented until midafternoon . . . when the drinking would start again.

Nothing seemed to help her. She had been shattered. The house became a prison of memories and dashed dreams. She couldn't explain any of it to anyone. And so, one evening, she simply decided to put an end to it all.

Was it an accident or intentional? No one truly knew. But on a cold November morning, less than a year after his dad's death, when his mom didn't answer her phone all morning, he and his wife went over to check on her. Her body was found in bed with a blanket pulled up under her chin. Her eyes were closed. She was wearing a pink nightgown. She looked peaceful. Almost relieved, it seemed to him. The doctors later told them that her death was caused by an overdose of pills and excessive alcohol. She just didn't want to be here anymore . . . without her first and only love. Time took its toll on her.

He thinks about time and aging. Then his mind goes back to his mom.

This sweet, funny, uncomplicated person was a victim of his dad's leap. She was so lost. He felt like a failure since he hadn't been able to help either one of them. What child could, he wonders?

How does it happen? How does it get so confusing? One moment his mom was a young bride and the next a widow deciding that life was not worth living. Do we control our destiny or are we mere pawns in some massive, cosmic mind game?

He wants to remember happier times. Vacation times. Family times. They did exist. They did count.

But life requires courage. Again, courage.

Life requires a brave heart. Life requires a commitment to push through the dark, sad moments.

Life requires love.

He tries to move his leg in the bed but cannot. He is just about done but feels he has to push on to find the answer to the riddle of his life. Or life itself.

There is a narrow window. It is such a small, narrow window. It is a window that opens to our destiny. So many choose not even to look through it. They live each day as if it was unconnected moments in time. They act as if choices do not have consequences. As if there is no cause and effect. Then again, others are frozen by the choice-and-consequence connection. Those are the ones that are frozen in time and space. They never live before they die. They just go from day to day trying to get through it. The majesty of the choices, the possibilities of consequences, the magic of one life seems to evade them.

That describes his brother to a tee. How come his brother stayed frozen in place? Kind of like a wooden carousel pony painted striking colors, but just going up and down and going nowhere? Nowhere. The Beatles song, "Nowhere Man," starts playing in his head. *How can you live a life and go nowhere?* he wonders.

His brother was younger than him. The kid was a good student. A pretty good high school athlete. But his brother decided to go right to work after high school. Mom and Dad tried to talk him out of it. He would not listen. *How is it that some kids just either think they know it all or just don't think at all?* He went to work at a small, local hardware store. His grand idea was to get an easy job, make a few bucks, live home, save up, and then travel around the world like some Marco Polo adventurer. It was pure fantasy, but the kid would not let go of that dream. Of course, life has a way of getting in the way of dreams.

One day at the hardware store, his brother was cutting some wood planks for a customer. He was gabbing away and not paying attention to the task at hand. The saw slipped from his grip. The cut sliced through his left arm. It severed the artery in his arm. There was blood everywhere. Although he put pressure on it and they called 911, the loss of blood was severe.

The consequence of so much loss of blood was a stroke. The stroke . . . this one slip at work . . . changed his brother's life. The stroke impaired his ability to read and write. It impaired his bowel control and the ability to simply take care of himself enough to do normal everyday activities on his own. His speech was dramatically affected, and his memory was limited. The dreams of his Marco Polo adventures were gone along with so much more. Yet, with loss came some unintended gains.

In an odd way, his brother became a gentler soul. Soft-spoken and so kind, especially to young children, he was a wonderful uncle to their daughter. His brother always found time to listen to her and seemed to understand her pain better than anyone else in the family. His brother was . . .

The hospital room seems busier now. It seems that there are more people in the room. He recognizes the different voices. It seems like they have come together for the final death watch. That last breath, the last possible revelation. One voice he hears is his brother's.

Since the accident, his brother's speech is slurred, his left cheek is drooping, and his ability to put words and sentences together is a challenge. He recovered from the accident but lived at home with their mom, worked behind the counter at the hardware store and taking the bus to and from home to work.

Since their mom died, he has lived in a state-run home for people who need some assistance in life.

Nothing ever really happened in his life. There was no traveling, no adventures, no loves, no next chapter. There was just each day the same. The same bus. The same lunch in the brown paper bag. The same small chatter. The same bus home. The same waves to different passersby. The same dinner in front of the TV.

The same old shows on the TV. A life is frozen in time like a carousel pony. Going around and around and getting nowhere. One moment. One choice. One consequence and the circle ride rides on.

What if? The what-ifs haunt all our lives. The turning left instead of right at the light. What if he paid a little more attention when he was sawing. What if he listened to mom and dad and went off to college? What if he was late that day to work and someone else had worked with the customer? What if that customer had decided to go to a different store or go on a different day? This sort of thinking is crazy making. Yet it is the story of every life.

Is that how he got here? Is that how he ended up dying in this hospital room? It was not supposed to be this way. This was not the plan. This wasn't even on the list of agenda items. Why didn't he go straight home this time? Why was he on a mountain road this one day?

The voices in the room have grown louder. *It is a bit annoying*, he thinks. *It is as if I am not even there.* Odd. *They are there to see me, yet it was as if I am not there.*

He hears his wife talking so sweetly to his brother.

It was hard for everyone after the saw accident. Mom and Dad were devastated. Their lives went in a different direction because of it. But they were solid in their support of their son.

He hears his wife say that she is going to go home and rest a bit. She says there is nothing more she could do. The hospital will call her if there is any change.

He is surprised to hear his brother tell her not to go. He says she has to stay. He tells her there is a narrow window and if she leaves it might close, and she will regret it forever.

She has grown quiet. She seems to listen to his brother.

She turns to look at her brother-in-law and asks, "A window?

Her brother-in-law says that all life is made up of windows, big and small—all narrow. All the good and bad things in life happen in the unexpected split second as a window opens or closes.

She says she will stay. "You're right. There is such little time left." She then asks, "How did this happen? Why was he on that road at that time of day? Where was he headed?" She shakes her head and puts it into her hands. "Why? Why now?"

His brother says that no one could answer that. He sure couldn't. Why anything at any one moment in time? Life just is.

They sit together and stare out the window into the night.

They fought the night before. It wasn't a bad argument. Just a disagreement about money. He resists thoughts of the argument. He knows he is dying and believes that the last thing you think about before you die is what you will take with you to the other side. Whatever that other side is he does not know, but he wants to play it safe anyway.

Money. *When did that take over all our lives? When did it start to consume everyone and everything? When did it start separating people from each other?* he thinks. Class barriers. Consumer choices. Lifestyle options. Money changes so many people. So many friends. Resentments grow. Jealousy. The stress of not keeping up with others. It takes on a life of its own. Cars. Houses. Watches. Clothes. Gadgets of all sorts.

He tried to fight the urge to acquire money solely as a lifestyle choice. But it became difficult as everyone else got caught up in it. He saw so many friends destroyed by either money itself or the desire for money. Money and things. Some friends let their families fall apart, and let their kids go off the rails in the constant pursuit of money. It happened in schools too. You could see it in the student's eyes. A sense of low self-worth all because of the type of clothes they wore or what advertisers convinced them they wanted though they could not afford it.

They had a very close friend who went into such a state of depression over not having the latest thing that someone else did that he had a total breakdown. This was a really bad event in the life of his friend's family and all their friends.

When was that? His mind races back to a day in 1996. It had to be in the fall. In those days, the new cars came out in the fall. The '97s were being put on the lots in the fall of '96. A whole bunch of friends went down to the BMW shop to check out the latest editions. His friend didn't need a new car and didn't really want a new car, but one thing led to another, and the salesman said something like . . . "This is not for everyone, only the select few." That did it. His friend signed the papers right then and there.

It was crazy. The man couldn't afford it, but something snapped inside him.

We heard later that he tried to return it, but that was a nonsense move. His friend's wife was furious. It was just another nail in the soon-to-be-filed divorce coffin. It was after that purchase that his friend's life fully unraveled. Everyone knew he was lost and afraid. He sold that car not long after he bought it, but it was too late to salvage his sense of pride in the age of shallow images.

He lost touch with that friend. He wonders, *What happened . . . ?*

All sorts of different images and thoughts are cascading through his head. They seem unrelated and yet followed a pattern of . . .

The nurse is back in the hospital room. His breathing is slow and heavy. Then, something so amazing happens. He opens his eyes. His eyes have actually opened!

The nurse calls out to his wife. His wife jumps up from her chair, comes over, and looks down at him.

Their eyes meet.

BREATH THREE

Who can really explain life and death? How to explain
time and aging? We can talk about it. We can write
about it. But can anyone truly explain them to anyone
else's satisfaction? Or even to themselves? We hear
doctors talk about the body and cells and organs and
their functions, and illness and disease and aging. We
hear philosophers pontificate about the meaning of life,
and spiritual thinkers talk about what happens at and
after death . . . but they never get down to the essence
of the why. The what is it all about. The how come. The
seeming absurdity of the human condition. Since
everyone dies anyway, what is it all about?

He opens his eyes. He wants to see the end. He wants to
see if it looks different at the end than in the middle. He

wants to know that if he keeps his eyes open, he will see something unique and special as his heart stops and his body fades into infinity. He wants to observe what others do around him when they believe he is gone. He forces his eyes to stay open.

The nurse is the first to speak. "Can you hear me?" are her first words. "Can you see me?" are her second words. He nods yes to both questions. "Can you say something?" is the next sentence. He shakes his head no.

At that moment, his wife looks into his eyes. He looks into her beautiful, sad eyes. He sees the tears in them. He hears her ask the nurse, "What does this mean?" The nurse says she does not know, but she has seen this happen many times.

His wife grabs his hand and holds it tight. She then leans down and kisses his forehead and his eyes. The tears running down her face fall onto his cheeks.

He takes his third breath. He understands that he has two left. He doesn't know how he knows. He just knows. What could he do with his sight in the next two breaths? How long is that anyway in the odd world they are all occupying now?

He realizes that they have all left the normal, everyday world behind and have entered a unique, spiritual world that does not follow the same rules as the living world. This is now the world of the near-dead. The rules are different. The images, sounds, voices, and perceptions are only available to those at this moment in time. We all know this truth instinctually, but no one ever says it. We enter a world that only a few recognize.

The near-death chamber of life. This is where life and death meet. This is where the ones who passed before can access the living realm. This is a portal for the previously departed to make themselves known again. It is as if it is a street corner where all meet one more time to answer questions, to ask questions, to reconcile old misunderstandings, to forgive, and to let go of anger so that you can move on in peace. The living. The dead. The spirits. The dreams. The memories. It is as if a field has been opened up to you that had been closed and hidden away for your whole life.

He squeezes his wife's hand. She shivers. She is ready for the journey. But before he begins his final walk to the other side, he pauses to consider how he and his wife have traveled together through the aging process.

Age.

It has always confounded him. When he looked in the mirror, he would see himself. He wondered if saw himself or a mental image of himself. *What do others see?* Some long ago image of an eighteen- or twenty-three- or even forty-two-year-old self? Is that the reflection that we see on our journey through each day?

There are days when we look in the glass window as we are passing a store and think we recognize the person in the window, but we don't. It is someone who is us and yet not. *Is that the person that others see which we only get a glimpse at periodically? Or do we all look different at different times throughout the day?*

Well, he decides, *either way, it is how one looks. Age takes its toll. The human machine wears down. Why is that? It does not seem fair.*

Then again, when did fair ever enter the equation in life? Life just is. It is not fair or unfair. Nature doesn't consciously choose what town to drop a tornado on, it just so happens that that town is there at the time of the tornado. Nature doesn't scheme as people do. The aging process is nature at work.

And throughout the entire aging in life, he and his wife hung together. The wrinkles. The gray hair. The loss of hair and hearing and eyesight, and on and on. Yet, when he looked at her, she looked the same to him as she did on their very first date.

Oh, he knew she was aging like everyone else. Like him. He saw and felt his softer belly and butt. Not quite what they used to be! However, he saw in her the girl he first met.

Maybe that is how it works. The first image of love is so emblazed on the mind that it colors all future images. Is that the magic of love? Is that what holds us all together . . . the imagination and the first look of love that effects all we see and feel from that first day on? He always saw—or *felt* is a better word—her inner beauty. Decency. A type of innocence you don't see too much today. She believes in people. She trusts that the better angels will win out in the end. Her belief structure simply makes her beautiful.

Interesting, he thinks. *What you believe changes how you look and how you see others.* At least it does for him when he looks at her. She was and is eternally bright.

He kept two photographs of his wife on his desk in his office. One was one from a few years ago when they were traveling in Hawaii. In it, she is standing on the back patio of a house they leased for the week on one of the small islands. She has a glass of red wine in one hand and is pointing out to the ocean with the other. She has a relaxed look in her eyes. Nothing was ever exuberant about any gesture since their baby died, but this image captured a look of appreciation in a moment of grace. The sand, the water, the blue sky, the beauty of the singular moment. She captured that look in her graceful pose.

The other picture was her when she was seven. It shows a young girl in a white-colored shirt. You can just tell that she spent time carefully picking out her clothes for this one photo. It defines *sweet*. She is all grins, and through the hopeful look on her face, communicates that life will be good and fair and kind. Her smile in that picture is authentic. It is the look of someone that feels everyone will be nice throughout the day and that tragedy would never target someone so sweet.

Life didn't turn out that way for her, or him, yet those pictures have kept him centered. The main feeling of both photos is of someone living in a state of grace. They're pictures of someone who wants to believe that goodness wins in the end.

For him, she has always stood for ageless living. For him, she has stood for youthful hope at any moment in time. Yet, through it all, time ticked away, the mirror was there, but the imagination kept them locked into the young boy and young girl who met, kissed, married, cried, and screamed at some of life's injustices, and still kept walking forward together.

Time. Age. Life. Death. Grace. Gratitude. Appreciation for even a moment of joy. We weren't promised any of it. In reality . . . we weren't promised anything. We shouldn't have expected anything in return for the gift of our lives. What were we thinking? We are no different than the trees, plants, and other creatures on the planet.

We are here, and life plays out. That's all. This thought slowly moves through and out of his mind. He felt a deeper and even more profound thought now enter him. Is this the final journey? The last two-breath journey?

Is there a place where past, present, and future meet? Is there a moment when time is no longer linear? Where time is no longer cause and effect? Where the rules are totally different? A place where you can go back and forth between experiences? A spot where life and death are here and gone. Where the dead come back, and the living die only to reverse it all a moment later?

Who can say? Why would we think we know it all when we truly know so little? Yes, we created the clock and the calendar, but who says we were even close to accurate in the grand scheme of the cosmos? You walk down a street. It seems like an average street in any town, but then it wobbles, it twists, it moves side to side and up and down. It vanishes and reappears. It changes form and color. It changes shape and direction. It goes straight up or straight down. It, in fact, is alive. It is a living breathing entity with a story all its own.

What if that road was time itself? What if time was a living breathing entity? A separate existence from any of us? What if it had its own story? Its own plot twists? What if it could reinvent itself and open doors to travelers to join it on a magical mystery journey? We really know so little. Yet time knows it all. It has seen it all over and over again.

Time is no longer merely a thing you keep count of like on the pages of a calendar or the hands on a clock; it is the reason for life itself. But first, you must understand that truth. Rethink the whole journey. Maybe, just maybe, if we can see time for what it truly is . . . a living entity with a journey of its own, we can go along for a ride we never conceived before. Maybe then we would redefine age. Redefine life itself. And definitely, redefine death.

Life, death, time. The present is here for a nanosecond. It is always fleeting.

He wonders if we ever really live in the present. Our minds are usually in the past or the future as we navigate the present fleeting nanosecond. We travel from the past to the present to the future in an unfolding wave of life. It is constantly in flux. And it also seems to be one big illusion. One massive sleight of hand by a master magician. So, is it really real or are we all in some trance that causes us to intersect with each other that is nothing more than someone or something else's dream state?

Is there a place where tangible and intangible meet? Where table and chairs—the tangible things in life— intersect with the intangible . . . with something you can't touch or taste or hear or see or smell that exists just the same? A thought? A feeling? A belief system? God? Time?

He remembers how much time he wasted worrying about things that either never happened or were not that significant anyway. Some things were big and important in his life: the death of his little girl, the loss of his dad and mom, his brother's accident, but now he wonders if, in this moment, they are reversible—or if not reversible, could he reenter time and have one more moment with his daughter and his mom and dad? Might he be given the gift of answers to questions and hear their voices again?

He is feeling a bit selfish now. He wants to seek forgiveness. He wants to seek absolution. In fact, he realizes that he needs to be granted forgiveness before his final exhalation.

He looks at his wife. She seems younger than just a few days ago when he was airlifted to the hospital. She has always been beautiful but never has believed it. That makes her even more beautiful. There is an ease to her beauty. Nothing threatening. She is what others called a natural beauty. He always thought that this meant that her inside beauty shone through. The inside overtook any slight blemishes on the outside and almost made the outside look better with the blemish. *Odd,* he thinks, *but true.*

He wants to know . . . if he holds her hand, will she go on the journey with him through time or is she just going to be a bystander puzzled by what he is doing and where he is going? Could the experience of death be shared?

He doesn't know that answer but has no choice but to press on.

He tries to squeeze her hand. She is surprised at how strong his grip is.

He cannot tell either way He just holds on tightly to her hand. He feels a wave of energy course through him, almost like an electric shock. It flows from his hand to her hand and then through her. Their bodies are acting as a conduit for life's electric current. The question is, what can pass through that conduit? What may emerge through time and space and enter both of them through the magic of the living time?

He can hear time beckon. He can sense a presence in their midst. He is alive with anticipation. Is it even possible? Is this the gift at the end? Is this the answer to the mystery?

He hears a voice. A little girl is calling out his name. No, it isn't his name.

He hears the word . . . *Daddy.* "Daddy."

It is said so softly. It is said with a mixture of love, childish excitement, hope, eagerness, and anticipation. He doesn't want to close his eyes yet, but he senses that if he doesn't he won't be able to connect with his baby.

He looks at his wife. He hopes she will understand that closing his eyes means they are getting closer and not further apart. He stares at his wife.

He now understands that if he closes his eyes, he most likely will never see her again. Never again.

How can he possibly leave this moment? He looks at her like he has never looked at her before. He studies her. He takes her all in. Her eyes, nose, lips, hands, fingers. Why don't we take the time to look at each other when we are just living the day?

She is magnificent. What a creation!

He thinks back to a Sunday morning, not long ago. It was about nine in the morning. He got up and put on some music. It was a song his dad used to listen to all the time. Perry Como's "It's Impossible." She smiled and rolled over to face him. She looked like a little girl. He saw his children in her eyes. He got back into bed, and they made love.

Their lovemaking was tender and gentle. He loved making love to her. He loved how her fingers knew exactly where to go and what to caress. He looked at her now and tried to give a slight nod, an acknowledgment of his appreciation of the time they chose to be together. But he knew he had to now leave. To close his eyes and connect on a different plain. He thought . . . *I will remember you. You made me better.*

It is as if she knows. It is as if she too understands that she was to be part of a grand experiment. That she is also to be a conduit. She stares at him.

She now realized that he would never see her again. Images flashed through her.

The first meeting, first date, first kiss, firsts of everything with him. The love, the anger, the heartbreaks, the joys . . . the . . . well . . . life. They took this journey together. She still believes it was right and true. She cannot think about her life without him. If nothing else, he made it all so dynamic and challenging.

She smiles. She looks at him and says, "Thank you. It was all worth the ride. Even though we faced such massive loss, we also embraced joy and love. No one gets out unbruised. No one gets out without loss and heartbreak. We should not have expected anything more or less. So, my sweet, thank you."

He watches as she closes her eyes first. He looks at her one more time. He only sees a child before him. That little seven-year-old girl with hope and excitement in her eyes. Then he takes a breath, looks around the room, looks up at the ceiling, says a prayer for illumination, and closes his eyes.

What does magic feel like? Not merely *look* like but *feel* like. When you see a magic trick, you watch it and try to figure it out but usually can't, even though it all seems so simple when you are shown afterward how it is done. Simple. Understandable. After all, there really is no magic.

But what if there was?

What if life itself is one big massive magic show? But put on by whom? Who is the master magician? Is this life a sleight-of-hand moment in time? Is there a greater force overseeing all of this? He remembers reading in Paul Brunton's book *A Hermit in the Himalayas*, where the author writes about the Overself. Is that where this thought is rising from? An Overself? Is it a separate being or part of who we each are?

He settled on the Overself. Is there One who watches over us all and can bend time and space? He doesn't remember much of Brunton's book, but the word *Overself* stuck with him. He always appreciated the concept of an overarching presence.

Linear is gone. Up and down are irrelevant. *High* and *low* just words created to help people describe things to each other. These are not real directions or relevant to anything or anyone. In this world he is now entering, is anything possible? But what of death? What is it? What happens? Where do you go? Where did you come from? The soul . . . is it real? What exactly is it? The personality. The essence of who we are. The life force. As these questions swirl around and throughout him, he knows that he is preparing for the last great adventure of his life—the last in all our lives.

The journey to the other world. The other side. The place we all dream about. The place we all fear. The place where we always were told there is no coming back from. And yet here he is. He is now in total unknown or even unknowable territory. Could the here and now and yesterday meet on a middle ground in this place? The place that exists between life and nonlife as we know it? He remembers being told stories of crossing over to another time and place when he was a boy—"come to Jesus" moments. Was this his? Do we all have one sooner or later? He could never relate to the idea before because he had never met someone resurrected. All he knows is that at night, deep in sleep, he was occasionally visited by the ones in his life who had passed on. Was that all mind games or was that the truth? Do the dead come back at night, in sleep, or in dreams? Or at time of death? Are there those who escort you over?

He hears music. It is a drumming. Kind of a shaman-type beat. There is a horn also. And a scratching type sound. Although it sounds odd, it is quite mesmerizing. Time is alive. Time is no longer a mere way of measuring the day or a life. Time is now also a living, breathing entity. *Maybe one day,* he thinks, *it will be discovered that we are just visitors in time's world.*

Time is now existing before him.

In fact, everything is alive and vibrating.

And that's when she enters. At the peak of all the sounds and vibrations she appears.

It is his little girl. She is as beautiful as he remembers. *Innocent* does not describe her. She is the child that created the word. It simply didn't exist until she entered the world. She is wearing a white robe. Not a long and flowing garment, but one that's just covering her body from shoulders to mid-calf. She has no shoes on. Her hair is pulled back, so her ears are visible. She seems slighter than he remembers. But there she is. She walks over to him on a staircase of energy. That sounds absurd, but it is the best way he can explain it to himself. He clutches his wife's hand. He can only hope that she is part of this miracle.

He hears himself say to her. "How?" There is no response. He hears himself say, "Please" and "Sorry."

It is then that he hears her say, "There is no sorry here. There is nothing to be sorry about, Daddy." He senses a tear rolling down his cheek. She then says: "There never was a here and there, Daddy. There is no here and there. There just is. People create all kinds of things, Daddy, to make themselves feel better or worse, but there just is. When we created here and there, by accident we created life and death. We began the separation from the complete story we all are to live and experience. We miss so much by the creation of this separation.

"Daddy, there is just a flow of energy in different forms and spaces. We are always here. We are always with each other. We never left each other, Daddy. I know we want to see each other, and you wanted to see me grow up, but sometimes some of us are just frozen in one moment in the past, and then that past is always the present for us."

What happens now? he wonders.

It is as if she has heard him. She says, "You will be given the gift of one day, Daddy. One day in the past to make it your present. Afterward, you will join us on this side. It is nice here."

He smiles at her choice of word *nice*. That is always what she said when she liked something. *Nice* was the biggest compliment she could give anyone or anything. *Nice* to her meant super-duper, great, spectacular.

And so here they are together in the past-present, that unique moment in time where life and death become one. Where all things are possible, and nothing is out of reach. This is the final gift to him from his Overself. A wish fulfilled. A dream realized. A personal moment of grace. A moment of reflection and redemption. A moment of forgiveness. A moment of the soul's resurrection. A place where anything is doable. This is where they are.

Was his wife with them? Or was this place just reserved for the dead and nearly dead? Were their hands touching enough to bridge the divide between life and death? Maybe he would never know. He hopes that his wife would be joining them on this last journey through the past-present. Maybe her presence would reveal itself along the way. There was no longer any time. It was suspended. The here and now was gone.

"Where do we go now?" he asks his daughter.

She says, "Let's go back to a happy time." That seems like such a childlike way to describe a day. *Happy.* But maybe that is all there really is . . . being happy or not. His mind is overwhelmed with what he is experiencing right now so he cannot think of anything. He thinks hard about what happy time his little girl is thinking about, but his mind is not bringing anything forward. She says any day can be considered a happy day if you want it to be. "Daddy, do you want me to pick a day?" He nods yes, and they are off.

He doesn't know now if this is real . . . whatever that means . . . or if he is just in his death phase of life and his mind is playing a last trick on him. He recalls hearing stories about how when people are close to death and their brain cells are "dying" from lack of oxygen and nutrients, their minds started hallucinating. Is that where he is now—in a hallucination?

Has he entered the chamber of illusions, fantasies, and wishful thinking or is there a real world that exists where the past and present meet? A world where life and death are mere mind games and nothing more?

Is there a dimension where life and death are interchangeable? He remembers his dad talking about the concept that maybe we are dead in our human lives on Earth and there comes a time that we enter life. We go to a place where everything is the reverse of all we have ever learned.

Whatever this trip in time is or isn't, he chooses to reengage with his little girl. Illusion or real, he wants to be with her again.

Although he doesn't know it, his wife is connected to them. How or why cannot be explained. But they are connected.

She is hearing all that they talk about. She cannot see what they are seeing but she can hear it as clearly as anything could be heard. She is feeling chilly in the hospital room and wants to go and grab a blanket, but she does not want to let go in fear of losing this connection. She holds on to his hand for dear life.

She hears her little girl take command of this incredible journey. She knew her little girl as a child, but right now, at this moment, her daughter is a fierce navigator in uncharted territory. How did this transformation take place? Where did it take place? The questions are many, the answers few. But the trip is before her. A trip back. Can they change anything?

She clutches his hand tighter still, closes her eyes and they are off.

He recalls the day well. It was summer. It was Sanibel. It was . . . could it be? It was the day his little girl died?

Why revisit that day?

She said they'd visit a happy time. How could that time possibly be happy? This is insane. He hears himself calling out to her to stop. Stop the journey. Rewind. Do something! He hears her giggle. Is she going to torment him? No! She wouldn't do that. So, what is happening here?

He hears her say. "Daddy, it is okay. It was such a happy day."

Even though they are merely observers of the day, it feels like they are reliving it also. There should be a feeling of separation from themselves on that Sanibel Island day but there isn't. They are present in the past as witnesses of the lives they lived. They aren't hovering over the events as much as just being spiritual forces embracing themselves and each other as the mystery unwinds itself before them.

They all know how the day ended. But their lives continued. Maybe that is how life itself is too. You kind of know how it all ends but you continue.

Wait! That's it!

The epiphany.

We all know how it all ends for all of us, but we continue anyway. We live, love, care, dream, and share life experiences in the constant shadow of death. Life takes courage.

Courage.

Why? He is focusing on the death. She is focusing on a day in a life. It is not about death. It is about the time in between. The in between. That is what it is all about. The in between.

He decides to just release himself into this last uncharted territory.

He feels like he was vanishing. He can hear his daughter but now is not sure if it is her then or now. The past is present and vice versa.

It was 6:30A.M. on that Sanibel morning. The house was quiet, yet he thought he could hear the kids downstairs desperately trying not to wake up Mommy and Daddy and failing miserably. The giggles were muffled, but with such a quiet house they echoed throughout. The children got out of their beds and decided, against their better judgment, to scurry upstairs and get into bed with Mommy and Daddy.

They got used to calling this time Willy Wonka time. That reference was to the Gene Wilder movie *Willie Wonka and the Chocolate Factory,* about the magical chocolate factory and a golden ticket.

They always laughed at the scene in the movie where Charlie, the little boy who is the hero of the story, sees all his relatives in one bed . . . parents and grandparents . . . all chattering away. The kids loved that scene and would shout out . . . "It's Wille Wonka time!"

And so, it was a Willie Wonka moment. They jumped into the bed, shouted out the magic letters . . . WW time . . . and woke up Mommy and Daddy. It is hard to get upset at moments like this, but his wife was always better at staying calm and present at these times than he was. She grabbed each of her precious daughters and hugged them, groggily saying, "WW time. Get over here, you chocolate bits! Cuddle with Mommy, my little cookies!"

He rolled over and said something like, "Really?!" But there they were. Together. One unit. One family. One moment. Was this the moment? Was this the happy time? Does it come down to spontaneous, joyful moments? Is that what life is? Just finding that one moment? And then they are gone. Like all things in life, the present is the past in a heartbeat.

After some more morning chatter, they all decided to go downstairs for pancakes, bacon, milk for the kids and coffee for the mommy and daddy.

Life is made up of small moments. It usually isn't the big things that stay with you. It is all the small, seemingly insignificant things that over time take on a life of their own.

The breakfast rituals, the smell of a morning cup of coffee, the aroma of maple syrup pouring out onto the pancakes. The sizzling of the bacon. The taste of the crispness of the first bite into that hot bacon strip. Even the sound of the plates on the table and the movement of the knives and forks seem to take on a meaning that he had never contemplated they could as the breakfast was unfolding. Why was that? *Probably,* he thinks, *because they seemed unimportant at the time.* He remembers how his mind was always focused on the "big" events in life, when, in fact, the big things were usually one and done, while the small things created the daily fabric of his life. The canvas that everything else was painted on.

Maybe that is what his little girl is saying. The big moments . . . even the tragic big moments . . . shouldn't obscure the texture of a life and the interplay between people who matter to each other. The texture. The canvas. It is not the quantity or size, but rather the quality and purity of life's events that matter.

And so, the day continues, except this time there are three invisible observers: his little girl, his wife, and him.

He watches how he went about his morning rituals. He is fascinated by the minute-by-minute movements of all of them. They were a kind of dance of sorts. All the movements of his family members had a flow about them that matched their personalities. He never realized that before but now it is so clear. Each had their unique dance movement. His little girls were like tap dancers, with constant up and down actions. Feet never stopping. There was a staccato-type pattern to their dance that embodied a Mister Bojangles' joy and exhilaration.

His wife was totally different. She was ballet. A graceful, fluid dancer. Long lines, arched back, hand gestures that seemed preplanned in the gentle rising and lowering of each arm or hand, or even, sometimes, her fingers. She was grace in action. She was beautiful. Yes, that's it . . . she was a swan in human form. He never really appreciated it before this moment.

He gets angry with himself for not seeing it earlier and commenting on it. Knowing her, she would have shrugged it off. With a flick of her wrist she would be saying, "Stop it."

And there he was. What was his dance in life? Not tap. Definitely not ballet. The best he can come up with to describe his movements as a dance, after watching himself all morning, is street hip hop- jazz type dance. A bit herky-jerky, but with his own offbeat style.

So, there they were. A dance company covering all the bases.

He watches the dances of each life. Somehow, they all match up. It is almost comical. A traveling dance troupe. A carnival. A circus of high-wire acrobats.

Suddenly, his attention diverts to the moment that has haunted their lives for decades. This time he sees it all differently. It was playing out in slow motion, like watching a play . . . a silent movie. . . a show being performed behind a silk screen, so you can make out the players and the movements, but like a shadow dance. He is frozen in place. But this time all of them are together watching. Yes, all of them . . . even his other beautiful child. Somehow, she too has entered into this dance of life and death. The entire family is together now in this past-present. His whole family is watching the event that tore each apart inside.

He feels a shift in the hospital room. The spell seems to be broken. Everyone in the Sanibel moment is fading. They're not gone yet but fading ever so slightly. Kind of like a flickering candle. He wills himself back to the past, and hears his little girl say, "Come back. Come back!" His back arches, and he forces himself to go back. He cannot lose this moment.

But it was not him losing the connection. It was his wife. She was trying to forget and didn't want to . . . or couldn't . . . relive this tragedy. He knows that with her or without her he has to go on.

Again, he remembers that he has heard that the last thing you say, do, or think before you die is the first thing you take to the other side. He needs to get this right. He needs to save himself at the end for a new beginning. He understands that that is why his little girl came back. She is his escort and wants to make the transition a good one.

He grips his wife's hand more tightly. This movement shocks her out of letting go. She instinctively realizes that this remembrance must happen. This moment must be relived if his soul, at the time of his death, is to find peace. She nods to herself in silence and quietly says yes.

Now the four family members are reconnected. It is as if by her reconnecting all four reconnected. She was always the glue in the family. That was always her unwanted role. And here she is, gluing them together once again. Maybe for the last time . . . the glue. The dance. The ballet of dreams.

They are all back in the Sanibel Island house. The moment is no more than a minute or two away. Can he change anything and bring her back?

No.

Can he stop time and figure out a way that it never happened?

No.

Can he command time to skip a minute . . . ten seconds . . . half a minute?

No.

So, what is the purpose of all this other than to torture him at the end? The fabric has been completed.

The tapestry has been finalized. The painter's last stroke is done.

So why?

His daughter says: "Life has to be seen as a bigger story than what is usually seen by most people. It is not some small tale of life, love, and death. It must be observed as the grand opera of massive proportions. Each life affects so many lives. Each life that is touched by another takes on some of the characteristics of the touched life. A life is never really lost. A life lives on in the hearts, mind, spirit, soul, walk, talk, touch, taste, sounds of all who came in contact with each other. You take the good qualities with you as you move forward.

"Daddy, we can't control death. Never could. Never will. It just happens on its own timetable. That is the lesson, Daddy. Death would have happened soon enough for any one of us in our wonderful family."

His little girl looks at him and quietly whispers, "That day I had the most fun I ever had on any one day. We laughed. We danced. We hugged. We shared. We sat together and ate pancakes with real syrup. We cared. We loved. We were one and that oneness stays. You were totally in the moment. Even if it was at the very end. Daddy, the end counts too."

She continues: "After that great breakfast and laughter, you went back upstairs. You disconnected. Everyone else began doing their own thing too. And then, it just happened. Daddy, you have so much more to learn about your life and your death before you come over. But once you do come over you will understand even more. So, let's look at it again, but differently now. Okay?"

He now realizes that he is in a whole different phase of his life and death. He better understands that although he is "talking" with his little girl, he is having a conversation with something or someone that is more than just one person. He is in a place where light and dark meet. A place where high and low and all the yin/yang elements of the daily routine evaporate. He senses that his little girl is the conduit for the Overself . . . and for GOD.

Is this experience the result of all the medicines in him or of a lack of oxygen? Does this happen to all of us as we wind down? Is it just a typical kind of illusion that naturally occurs at the time of our death?

Whatever it is, it feels real and is happening in real time. So, he chooses to let go of his skepticism and let the experience in. It is the last experience of his life. And it might just shape his death.

His daughter's voice changes a bit. It takes on a more authoritarian tone. An all-knowing, been there, seen it, even created it all tone. So, who is he to deny access to his heart and soul to whatever is happening. He hears himself whisper, "I am letting go of all fear and doubt."

He senses a bright light around him. It is not only all around him but feels like it is inside of him too. He is the light. It feels like his body has vanished and he is all light and energy. He wonders if he is now gone from the world he always knew. He is both confused and excited. He doesn't remember being this exhilarated for so long, if ever. Clearly, he has not been this exhilarated since his daughter's death. Since her death he has carried a sadness with him that blanketed everything he did. But now he is light. He hears music of some sort. And so, he lets go.

His daughter says, "The life you live is not the only life playing out as you walk the earth. You are more than the sum of your parts. There is a part of you that cannot be calibrated by science or doctors or x-rays or scans. It is that part that is the essence of life. The essence of being. The connecting tissue to the larger story. You see we are all connected. We are all living the story of the human condition. We all affect each other. That is why we must help each other. By helping each other, we are helping ourselves. It is not selfish to assist yourself because we are all one. It is all one. We are all pieces of the Overself.

"The life you are given is fragile, frail, and easily dissolvable. But it is not the whole story of your time here. Here. Now. Then. Past. Present. Future. These are just concepts and not the story of who we are."

She continues, "When did you lose sight of that? When did you forget the meaning of life? Daddy? Think about it. Life is amazing!"

He thinks that she sounds both profound and childlike. And maybe that is the answer. Maybe profundity and innocence are joined at the hip, so to speak.

She goes on, "Life is this gift that is beyond gifts. It is bizarre how we treat it like it is a given. It is not. We toss it around, treat it so shabbily, abuse it, and many times mock it. And sometimes we voluntarily give it back! Crazy, Daddy. Why would you give up a once-in-a-lifetime life?"

A once-in-a-lifetime life, he reflects. That sentence lingers in the air around him.

"But what of the death of a child?" he hears himself saying to his daughter. "I never got past it. I was frozen in that moment of loss. I missed you so much I could hardly bear it.

"No, remove the adjective *hardly.* I could not bear it. It destroyed who your mother and I were and what we could accomplish. I fear it led to my being here right now. My dying right now. It is all connected. The grief has been suffocating."

He feels her little hand take a tight grasp of his. He senses they are all together again. His daughter says: "I know you wanted to be with me longer and be at my birthdays, graduations, wedding, first job, grandchildren births, with me for all the joys of life, but life is more than that. We are not merely lengths of time. We are not merely holidays and special days like those. Daddy, we are movement, thoughts, hopes, dreams, memories, wishes. . . . We are intangible. You see, everyone thinks we are only tangible. Only solid things you can touch. Like a table or a chair. But that is only a small percentage of the whole story. We are, if we choose to be, much, much more. We are intangible. And an intangible thing can never dies, never go away. The intangible stays forever—or at least as long as you wish and will it to.

"And that, Daddy, is the secret. The gift of gifts. The life of a life. So, you can let go of me, but I am all around you always. It is not pretend. It is not make-believe. It is not wishful thinking. It is the truth behind the curtain. The solving of the mystery.

"So now, let's move forward. Don't grieve. Yes, I have been frozen in time in some ways, but I am forever with you, growing and living in a world that I could not share with you before this moment.

"Why is it at the end that the meaning of life is realized? The purpose of a life is not to see who stays here the longest. Rather, it is to understand that it is all a blink of an eye and therefore each moment must have meaning. Each moment must be lived with love in your heart. Each moment is the only moment. And then . . . it is gone.

"Daddy, it was simply life playing out that day. No one's fault. No one's mistake. We all live. We all pass through. But for one bright, shining moment, we were one. So many never even get that.

"It is not the beginning and not the end that count . . . it is the middle part of life. And that middle part was wonderful! What more could anyone ask for? I am grateful I was your daughter. I love you, Daddy.

"So, Daddy, it is now time to go back to see how you got here and what happens next. I have to go. I am going to let go. It is okay though. I am always around and soon we will travel together again. But for right now, there is work you must do and finish. Solve the mystery of the path you took on the mountain road."

How? How is that even possible? he thinks.

"You just have to trust," she replies. "Take this moment to finally see the meaning of it all."

With that, his little girl lets go. He feels his wife's hand release his also.

He hears his other daughter let go. And he finds himself alone again. He is exhausted. He has to figure out what has happened to him and them.

He has to come to terms with his life and death before the last breath.

BREATH TWO

If it is true that new beginnings can come at any stage of life, does that also mean that new beginnings can come at the end of a life?

That idea sounded like the ultimate oxymoron to him. But if what his little girl had said was true, then maybe learning the answer would be part of figuring out the puzzle of life. Life events seemed random to him. His mind was rocketing now from image to image in different stages and phases of his life.

His mind takes him back to the day before this now-dying moment. The day was like any other day. He got up and made his usual breakfast: coffee, granola, and a banana. He took all his prescribed pills, brushed his teeth, gave himself a quick look in the mirror, and put on his workout clothes. Funny how he always took a quick look in the mirror. It seemed that the older he got, the quicker the looks in the mirror were.

His wife was still sleeping, although she was starting to make movements to acknowledge that the morning was there. Her day usually started about a half hour to an hour after his. He kissed her forehead, transferred the coffee from the coffee cup to the carry-out thermos, and grabbed a bottle of water from the fridge. He started the car from the remote control "key" so that the car would be warm and the music was on when he got in it. He was still a fan of the oldies. Those same songs seem to bring comfort to him. The familiarity of it all set a calm tone for his morning drive to the gym.

"I Believe" was playing on the CD player as he opened the car door. That particular song had soothed him over the years. Believing. Believing that with every tragedy a new hope is born. Something about believing in this concept of birth after death kept him relatively sane after the loss of their little girl.

He sang the song out loud as he drove to the gym. The fifteen-minute drive let him play it twice before he switched over to his other must-hear morning song, "Now and Forever." He parked the car and joined the morning workout gang. Usually it was the same group, with a few exceptions, at this time of the morning. He worked up a good sweat and then was going to head out for a second cup of coffee before going home. Normally, he would shower, put on jeans and a sweatshirt, and start the day. What made him deviate yesterday from his routine? Why didn't he head straight home? For some random-seeming reason, he had decided to head to the mountains.

He shifts his body slightly in the hospital bed. He is being tormented by his decision. His choice. No one else had been there.

His mind goes blank. It is as if the little oxygen circulating in his bloodstream is slowly sapping him of his last thoughts and dreams. He shakes his head to try to reconnect, but it doesn't help. His mind travels in a totally different direction.

He is now with his mom.

When was this? He tries to squint to see better, as odd as that sounds. There he is, sitting on the edge of a car bumper. It was an old car. Light blue. Convertible. Where was it? That's it. Lake George. Upstate New York.

The car was outside a cabin at some lakeside resort. He was sitting next to his mom on the car bumper. He could not be older than four. His mom was so young. Probably half the age he is now, dying in a hospital bed a thousand miles away from that lake. A thousand miles. A lifetime away. A dream ago. His mom was funny, though with a sadness about her. She wasn't school smart; she was street smart. Today they would probably call her clever. They didn't use that term back in the 1950s. But that's what she was. Also, funny—but with sad eyes.

He thinks about how common that is for so many people. Their funniness covering over a basic sadness because of knowing how futile and fruitless it all is. This whole life thing is just bizarre.

There he goes again. The . . . what? What does he have to do here to right something before his last gasp? He has to say sorry . . . again. It seems he is spending his last minutes always saying sorry to someone about something.

Maybe that is just the way it has to be? We have to make amends for our human condition. Don't we all seek forgiveness sooner or later?

He looks at himself. Is that where he was driving? Is that where he turned off to go up the mountain road? Is this another moment he must visit to seek forgiveness and say he feels sorry? But say sorry to whom? And for what, this time?

His mind goes back to the image of him being four and sitting next to his mom. He had a look like the sun was in his eyes. He had a kind of downward glance. He remembers how he loved his mom. He never told her enough. She needed to hear it, but he was too young and self-absorbed to know enough to say it. Why was that?

Why do we test the ones we don't need to test in a relationship? Why can't we give each other a break? Why can't we love with abandon and just give in to the feeling of appreciation? Are we afraid of looking weak? Of feeling dependent? Of losing control of some part of ourselves? It was his mom . . . for Christ's sakes!

Lake George. Innocence. Simplicity. Nature. What he would give for one more moment with his mom. If he had known how things would turn out for his mom, would he have, even at four years old, been more attentive to her and this moment?

Life doesn't work that way. We are always wiser when looking back! Maybe he would be with her soon. Yet it won't be the same. It was that moment in time. It was that experience. It was that life. It was them in that moment. That moment!

That is what it was. That one moment.

Again, he concluded, *the in-between moments are the ones that seem to matter.*

He wanted to stay there at age four in Lake George with his mom sitting on the car bumper. But the moment was gone in a flash—just like moments always are.

In a flash, he is in his car. He is back on the mountain road now.

And why did he turn off the usual route from gym to home? He can't remember. *Who can really ever explain why we do what we do? Sometimes something deep inside just carries us away in a direction that we never intended.*

There he was . . . not turning right onto State Road 119 as was his routine. Instead, he headed up Highway 36 West. He reached the turnoff to Ward. He took it. It's strange to revisit this memory.

His mind is kind of blank. It is drifting randomly over events in his life. In no linear fashion.

Days going to the shooting range with his dad when he was about nine. His dad loved to collect rifles and go

PAUL R. LIPTON

to the rifle range to take target practice. He didn't care for it that much, but he liked those Sunday mornings with his dad. He enjoyed feeling like it was a "guy thing." His dad would introduce him to the other men at the range and say, "This is my son." He liked that.

His mind then rockets to another time and place. He was now sitting with his mom watching an old movie at home on a Saturday afternoon. He was probably twelve. His mom loved old movies and wanted to tell him about all the different actors and actresses and what other movies they were in. He figures that this is what hooked him on being a movie lover himself. It wasn't so much the movie as it was a comforting moment of being a kid with his mom on a Saturday afternoon.

But then . . . like flipping a page in a flip chart, he was in junior high school heading to math class, and then . . . high school in Driver's Ed feeling excited about his chance to drive a car.

Car.

He was back on that mountain road now. His car was just entering Ward, a truly funky little spot. Old VW buses. Peace signs. A coffee shop and a glass-blowing studio with some houses and old cars and trucks thrown into the mix. He was going to stop, but decided to head over to Nederland.

Nederland . . . another town from a different time. Yoga retreats, crystal shops, a variety of unique eating places, and people who are trying to escape the modern extravagances of the day.

He pulled into the Kathmandu restaurant. He didn't know why. Probably because the name brought him back to his time spent in Kathmandu, Nepal. What a time that was.

He remembers trekking up the mountain paths on his way up to the monastery at Tengboche. He wanted to be part of the mountain. He wanted to understand life and death. He hoped that he would witness some awakening in himself. The meaning. The purpose. His wife was right by his side on that trip. She too was seeking answers to death. And more specifically, the death of their baby girl.

He remembers sitting with the monk. The mountain was like Mount Baldy and also different. They were alone on this mountaintop in the middle of Nepal. He so needed to feel an opening to knowledge. . .

And now he was back in Nederland.

He grabbed a coffee and some late breakfast, early lunch . . . *brunch.* That's the word! There was no phone service up there, so he might as well have been in Nepal again.

What was he doing? He had finished eating and turned his collar up as he walked out into the brisk mountain air. He had sat in his car a bit and then decided to head past the Eldora ski resort and take Coal Creek Canyon down to Boulder. There were tears running down his face as he started his car. He didn't know why. But he was quietly sobbing. As he drove alone through the canyon, he had felt a chill run through him. *This is it,* he had thought. *This is life.*

He changed CDs and started playing Dan Fogelberg's "Leader of the Band" and then "Run for the Roses."

This is what life comes down to. Sooner or later, you travel alone through the canyon . . . . The twists. The turns. The surprises. The edge. The loneliness of a singular life with the thoughts of a lifetime about all the losses and the errors in judgment that build up over time. They are like a ball of twine gathered together that then starts rolling down a massive mountain.

Eventually it just all unravels. A lifetime is spent creating the ball of twine. Choices. Decisions. Judgment calls. False starts. Hurts. Cuts, Bruises. Loved ones gone too soon. Innocence lost. Hope drained. And yet we keep going. Why?

We keep trying. Why?

We keep wanting to make it right. We so desperately need to find an answer for any of it. And all along the trip, the clock keeps ticking. The calendar days keep vanishing. The lessons learned are lost. The ones you thought were heroes are shown to merely be human like you. Then the ball of twine keeps rolling down and keeps getting smaller and smaller. It is as if it, and you with it, is vanishing.

The years spent acquiring stuff are now spent discarding the same stuff. Until. Until what? Until it is all gone, and it can never be created again . . . not in the same way . . . because the twine can never be rewound in the same pattern ever again. One unique ball of twine wrapped just right for each life. One life. One time. One story. One tale forever lost in the history of time. Just unraveling through the ending years of a life.

The ending years. That was the nonsense of it all. The end can be after a day or a hundred years. It can be as a five-year-old little angel or a sixty-four-year-old man lost in thought on a mountain road.

He realized that it was not the years that counted but just the one day. It all always comes down to one day. Whether we are a baby, a young child, a young adult, or someone older, life begins and ends in one day. Between birth and death, if a connection is created between people, they live inside one another. We carry the lessons of the people we love with us. Their story. Their history. We are entwined with them as part of our ball of twine. They are never gone.

As he was driving, he had begun to feel illumination. An awakening. He thought he was finally getting to the point of it all. A ball of twine. Wind it up, create it, and then unravel it. It was okay. It was the way it was for us all. Age was irrelevant. Time was an illusion. The singular moment was the story told. He had wanted to get home to tell his wife and his daughter. An excitement like he hadn't felt in years had overcome him.

He was so lost in thought that he had let his car drift to the right and the edge of the canyon. He tried to pull it over to the center but overcompensated. The car hit the left wall of the canyon, then bounced over to the right again, and this time the front wheels had missed the road and edged over the lip of the canyon. He remembered the sensation as the car was slipping further over the ledge.

He shakes in the hospital bed. He now realizes he has at least one broken arm. He now feels the cast. He now senses his left leg elevated. *What happened?*

He now sees his mom and dad standing over him.

These images no longer shake him. He understands he is dying and that all that has happened had to happen. It just did. His mom and dad look at peace. He hears them both say, "You're okay. It is okay. We all do the best we can, son. Remember, it is not just what is said and done but why that matters. The intention behind the what and the why. Son, your intentions were always good, decent, and honorable. We all fail in the end to complete the story of our lives, but that is part of the life story."

He looks at them both. He feels calmer than he thinks he should be. Then he hears them say that he needs to take two answers with him as he transitions over and as the ball of his twine unravels. "Son, carry these two thoughts with you. First, after death there is no more pain or suffering on any level. It is like you begin fresh. Take that thought with you.

"And second, you were courageous in life. You tried your best to be noble in all the things you did and said. You believed. Take comfort in the courage you exhibited in the face of the efforts of those who totally lost their way and tried to derail you from your path. That includes you too, son. We so often self-sabotage our own journeys. Forgive yourself, son."

With those words, they slowly dissolve before him. They are gone, and he is left lying there in his hospital bed feeling more at peace.

Does the lesson have to come at the end? Is that how it happens?

Does life only make sense backward?

We live it forward. We have no choice. But, in the end, maybe we are given the gift of seeing it in all its glory the way it was intended . . . backward.

As he lays dying, the rest of the world keeps right on spinning. For some reason, we all kind of think that maybe it doesn't. Our egos so desperately want to believe everything begins and ends with our personal story. But it is just not that way. The graveyard is filled with the corpses of rich and famous people who truly thought that everything swirled around their singular stories. And maybe it did for a bit. Then the story ended and years later no one even knew who they were. You would end up Googling them and wonder what the fuss was all about. Kings, queens, actors, stars, writers, politicians, and so. Too often they are not even on the minds of the ones who once knew them. And soon, the ones who knew them are gone as well and there is just a blank stare when one of their names is mentioned or read.

In his opinion, there are three times that a person dies.

The first time is the physical death. The actual loss. The body. The tangible being. The face, the touch, the look, the personality.

Then there is the second death. Usually, when the funeral service or gathering to talk about a friend or cousin or business partner who is gone ends, it is like a death. Stories are shared. As are laughs, tears, and funny or clever comments. Maybe how the ones left behind were changed for the better or worse because of the life that has just ended is discussed. It is like sitting around a campfire and telling tales of bygone days. What they were like, the adventures and misadventures of the life just gone. After that, the person is let go.

But it is the third death that has always caused his mind to do flips.

The third death is the one that haunts most people.

The third death is when you are no longer on anyone's mind at all. You are finally forgotten. There are no stories. No campfire tales. No nothing. You are lost like so many clouds passing across the sky. You look up, see the cloud, comment on its shape, color, movement, and then it is gone. It was unique for a moment.

A cloud may have caught your eye for a moment. It even may have captured your attention and imagination for a moment, but then you looked away, and when you looked back up into the sky, it was gone, and you may not even remember seeing it in the first place. Another cloud formation has taken its place, which now garners your attention.

The third death.

Is the third death the reason we do the crazy things we do sometimes? We so much want others to remember that we were here? He thinks, *How bizarre that is, wanting to control the memories of others. It is an impossible task. And it doesn't matter. Really, who cares? But we seem to all reflect on this.* At least he is still doing it . . . even with his last few breaths.

He wants to say that maybe the answer to the riddle of the multiple deaths we all transition through is that we realize that we have a life, a moment, and we have to be "good" with it. Ourselves. Alone. Just be good with the life we have lived, the lives we have touched, and the difference we made as we went through each day. Period. Maybe the story is no bigger or grander than that, but that is pretty good standing alone.

Or maybe the bigger, grander story is that if each person lives a good, honorable life, then we are all the better for it . . . whether or not any one of us is remembered.

So maybe that is why we have to live a life that tries to help, not hurt. That tries to give and not merely take . . . that wants to love with abandon and not hold back from connecting with another. Just maybe that is the answer to the third death.

His mind is getting weary and cloudy again. He wants to go to sleep but realizes he cannot. Going to sleep now means going to sleep forever. He wonders if you dream as you drift to the other side. The last great adventure into a spot that we all go to, but from which no one, as far as he knows, comes back from. But maybe that is not so . . . Else how to explain his "time" with his little girl and his mom and dad?

It is just all too much now. These thoughts are just too esoteric for him especially at this moment when he wants to go back to his life and the life of his loved ones. He causes himself to snap out of this thought string.

Seated in the hospital room beside the bed, she is watching him the whole time he is dancing with his third death thought. She wonders if he is thinking or dreaming about anything or if he is totally unconscious. She figures, *Wherever he is now, we will all be there soon enough!*

She wants to remember happier times. She wants to laugh again. She wants to stop feeling bad—even at this moment. She recalls what he said about the importance of finding joy in even the harshest of moments. When she used to ask him what he meant by that—since it sounded so paradoxical—he would simply say that in the end you want to feel life and the magic of it even if it is a moment of pain and anxiety. Because life is a unique gift that is here and then gone. She decides to take him literally, at his word, so she looks down at him and smiles.

She recalls her close-to-death moment.

It was about two years ago. It was early in the morning when a sharp pain brought her to her knees as she was brewing coffee. He saw her fall. She was as white as a ghost and in more pain than he had ever witnessed before. He got her to the car and rushed her to the emergency room.

She stops herself in the midst of this memory and looks around the scene to see where she was at that exact moment. It was the same hospital and only perhaps a room or two down from where they are now!

She was put on an IV and given a lot of pain medication, and then she drifted into a deep, medicated sleep. All she knows is what they told her after the surgery. A blood clot had formed in her large intestine and she was dying. Her vital signs had dropped to barely functioning.

He had watched helplessly as the doctors took her in for emergency surgery. Although they removed over 60 percent of her large intestine, they saved her. The recovery was steady and solid until the incision started leaking. She was taken to the ICU and then had a second surgery. That night she had hung on for dear life. Staying alive was truly a matter of will.

Friends and family gathered to either give her support or be there to help the family if she didn't make it through the rough night ahead. But due to her positive attitude and generally healthy body, she made a full recovery.

That was a close call. What she recalls most now about it was the love and commitment he demonstrated to her and her recovery. It was unconditional. Whatever doubts she'd ever had if he would be there for her vanished. That clot and double surgery brought them even closer together . . . if that was possible. She remembers that time now, oddly, with fondness. It was a pure moment of dedication by one man for one woman.

It felt like he had finally fulfilled his wedding vows in that hospital emergency room and recovery.

She smiles and says, "You crazy boy . . . you were right all along. We must find the majesty in a life . . . even in the moments of illness and death. It is those moments that bring out the humanity and devotion that we have for one another."

Death.

The ultimate hat trick. You are laughing, eating, drinking, loving, crying, sharing, dressing, brushing your teeth, combing your hair, and then it's gone! In a blink of an eye. Gone. The absurdity of it all.

She laughs out loud. She puts her hands over her mouth to muffle the sound and then just cracks up. She feels as if he has given her the last great present of all the presents he had ever given her.

The gift of knowing.

Life is this combination of joy and sadness, laughter and tears, fear and bravery, love and disappointment . . . It is all wrapped up in a bundle and then gone. She realizes that laughter is an important part of any life.

He hears her laughing. It makes him feel good. He loves her laugh. It is one of those contagious ones. He feels he knows what she was experiencing and he is so grateful that he was there for her when she most needed him.

The basement of his childhood home pops into his mind.

The basement of the house was always spooky to him. It was unfinished and packed with cartons filled with one thing or another. There were also shelves along the walls that contained the leftover, forgotten, half useable, partially broken things acquired over the lifetimes of all the family members in the house. The furnace was also down there.

As a young boy, the furnace always scared him. He didn't know why, but it always did. Maybe it was the sounds it made or just the way it looked—like some kind of hulking creature that was not alive but could come alive at any moment. He rarely, if ever, went down there and when he did he wanted to get out of there as quickly as possible. Maybe it was also that one movie he watched as a young boy that kept him from going down there.

As a youngster, he saw *The Incredible Shrinking Man,* a wonderful science fiction movie about a man who starts shrinking after going through some mysterious cloud while on a boating trip. He gets smaller and smaller until he finds himself in the house basement fighting a huge spider that wants to devour him. The battle with the spider is set in the cluttered basement. Maybe it was that scene in the movie that got his young boy's mind spinning. Basements, clutter, spiders, and a battle to the death. Yet, after the shrinking man kills the spider, the man has a revelation. This shrinking, vanishing man steps through the smallest opening in the screen covering a window and looks up at the stars. The disappearing man finally realizes that he is not small. And he is not disappearing. He is merely changing form and substance. He is not big or small. He just is, and he matters, no matter his shape and size and form. He is one with the universe. He has lived and will continue to live in some place and time and space.

We never really disappear. We may change form and may change our makeup, but we do not vanish. We join the amazing, expanding cosmos. We become one with nature and everything else that lived and existed on Planet Earth.

Isn't that crazy, he thinks. *Humankind always saw itself as superior to all other creatures and beings . . . whether plant or animal . . . on this planet, yet in the end, we all come together in the ebb and flow of energy and the cosmic story of life and existence itself.*

Is that it?

He shifts in the hospital bed.

Throughout his early years spent living in that house with his mom, dad, and brother, he never liked going down into the basement.

But his dad did. Beside all the boxes and clutter, his dad set up a workbench. Quite a setup for that time. He had vises, saws, and every type of gadget you might find at a hardware store. His dad took great pride in them all. On Saturdays or Sundays, his dad would go down there and make stuff or fix stuff. He made lamps out of beer mugs. He made picture frames. Small projects like that. But then his dad took up painting. He was self-taught. His dad started painting portraits and discovered the artist within. His dad's paintings got better over time. The shading and facial expressions became subtler and more meaningful. But then, like some whirling dervish, his dad wanted to take up photography. It was as if he wanted to say that he was not merely what he did for a living. He was going to define himself bigger, more, and be a creative force. His dad was silently crying out to be seen and heard for more than the working guy. His dad knew nothing was wrong with that, but he just wanted to express more . . . even if just in a basement of the family house.

There is both a sweetness and a sadness to it all, now that he is looking back on his dad's artwork. If he'd only appreciated his dad's efforts at the time. His dad so much wanted to be acknowledged as more . . . even if just to his little family in the basement of this small house.

He wonders how many men and women hide away their talents and gifts in the basements of their minds and souls. He wonders what they are waiting for before they will unleash their talents and gifts? He knows that he too has never expressed his full potential. Why was that? He cannot find a suitable answer to the question.

But his dad kept at it in that basement.

Then, one day, his dad converted part of the basement into a darkroom and took up developing his own pictures. He got a kick out of taking the pictures, developing them, and proudly showing the family the final product of his imagination and creation. But as a young boy with other things on his mind, he never really gave his dad the kudos he deserved for his artwork. What he would give to go back and be more appreciative!

Project after project. His dad was proud of them all, yet he also saw that his son seemed to care less. His son never sat by his dad's side to learn, to watch, to connect, to try to understand.

The pain of not appreciating another's efforts runs through his body now. Another tear wells in his eyes as he lies dying in his darkened hospital bed.

In his mind, he calls out to his dad. He is seeking forgiveness. But forgiveness for what? Maybe for being a self-absorbed kid? But aren't all kids like that? It has to be something more than that. He keeps twisting the images in his mind. Maybe it is for never ever wanting to take the time to understand his dad better. To just sit by his side and take in his dad's story. His dad's gifts, talents, dreams, shattered wishes. Maybe that is why there has been a hole in him all these years. There is a vacant space where his dad's story should have resided. Was his dad angry or upset by his son's lack of interest? Was that one of the causes of his dad's tragic end? It had to be more than that . . . right? He is so confused. He just knows he has to forgive himself.

Forgiveness. Is that what life all comes down to? Not merely forgiveness from another but forgiveness from yourself to yourself. Again, self-absolution. Self-cleansing. Washing away the flaws and errors that fill our lives. Maybe that is why he has been lingering here: to work it out and absolve himself from himself. Is that the final lesson in life? The death class. The death homework assignment. The death final exam. In the end, maybe judgment day is facing yourself and grading your own life effort. There is no grand biblical moment. instead you face yourself for one final evaluation in an effort to achieve a sense of personal peace.

He realizes that all through his life he has longed for peace.

Peace of mind. Peace in the whirling mind of thoughts, regrets, dashed everything. Yet peace of mind seems so hard to achieve. *Why is that?* he thinks. Maybe peace of mind is connected to wants and needs and expectations about life and what should happen or should have happened. Maybe peace of mind is just an illusion. It feels so often that his mind has a will and a life of its own. He tried meditation. He tried mindfulness. He tried yoga and various breathing techniques to quiet his mind. They all worked for moments but not in the long term. His mind always raced along. He worried a lot. He fretted too much. The fretting was not about big stuff or even stuff that would naturally happen. It was just about stuff . . . big or small didn't matter.

Maybe we are all like that. Worry may just be part of the human condition. If that is the case, then maybe we just need to accept worry. Embrace it as part of who we are, sigh about it, smile, look up, and move on.

He hears noise in the hospital room. It breaks this spell. He cannot make out the source of the sound at first. Then he realizes that it is more doctors coming into the room. He hears some chatter about whether there should be an autopsy.

Autopsy?! Of him?! Why? What exactly happened to him that brought him here?

He remembers the road, the car, the falling but he doesn't want to be autopsied! Then he thinks it wouldn't matter much or would it? Some doctor studying the why and how that caused his death. He hears his wife ask if it is necessary.

Good girl, he thinks. *You ask those questions!*

The doctor told her it is not legally required but asks, doesn't she want to know how and why this sudden tragedy happened. He doesn't hear her response but only hears the doctors say okay and walk out. Did she approve it?

She leans over him and whispers into his ear, "Rest in peace, my love. No one is cutting you up. I don't need to know the why and how. I just wish you were here and we could grab coffee together one more time."

Oh, how they will both miss the simple routine moments of life. Especially, a morning cup of coffee and an after-dinner ice cream sundae with whipped cream and hot fudge!

He feels his body melt a bit more into the hospital bed. He thinks about the seasons of life.

He wanted to be a man for all seasons. He wanted to be fully developed and well rounded. It didn't play out that way, but he tried. Over the years, he read all kinds of books on religion and philosophy. He studied art and the masters. He traveled to experience different cultures, and he learned to enjoy the simple moments in life—the moments that usually escaped most others became his central focus. He would find himself staring at flowers or sunsets or trees and birds for the longest time and wondered why he would do that. But then he realized the basic answer: He knew this moment eventually would come . . . death . . . and sensed that the one thing he would like to do one more time was to witness the simplicity of what life could be.

God created it all. So why not take the time to appreciate it all? That is what always puzzled him about his friends. They seemed to focus on everything but the beauty of the individual moment of the glory of the clear vision of life in action. The bird on the wing. The flower in bloom. The trees living in harmony with its surroundings.

Harmony. The word echoed inside him. We seem to have lost harmony. The ebb and flow of life. Appreciating the glory in harmony. Especially in relationships. *Oh lord,* he thinks, *the incredible disharmony that exists in all relationships.*

This thought takes him back to her again. Her and his harmony and disharmony! It seems that the disharmony was more in the early years than the later ones. *Why is that?* he wonders. Maybe it was the striving in the early years that interrupted the ability to relax into a more textured, easy flowing, harmonic relationship.

His mind takes him back to their separation. It was a time of massive upheaval and unrest for him, her, and the whole family. The whys and how-comes seem irrelevant now. It is hard to put your finger on any one reason. But now, as he lays dying, he realizes that it was fear that caused it all.

That nemesis.

Fear.

It seemed to surface in his life at fairly regular intervals. Every few years, the fear of either age or time passing or failure to succeed in some venture or job resulted in a crashing of the fragile harmony in his marriage and family life. It was painful and hurtful. It was as if he had lost all sense of sanity during these momentary spasms of his soul.

He is so grateful looking back over his life that she was who she was and fought through and past the insanity that galloped through their lives during those moments. They became best friends. Maybe it is true friendship that can see all the flaws and love anyway. Whatever their source, he marveled at her strength and commitment to their life together.

And so here he lays. Seeking harmony. Seeking a rhythm. Seeking a natural flow of energy. Odd he thought. Seeking harmony at the time of death. Talk about futility. Or is it?

We are given this moment in time. So why not live it fully until the very last breath? Whether anyone else knows it or not, he understands now that it doesn't matter. So long as each one of us finds it, isn't that enough? Maybe that is the way life itself should be. No showboating. No waiting for applause. No celebration. Just an inner knowing that you . . . alone . . . singularly . . . in isolation . . . are good with yourself.

But then, he thinks that before that harmony can be you have to forgive yourself of your failures, weaknesses, betrayals, regrets, and every other negative moment in your life that you brought on yourself. Is that what this dying process is all about? The journey to personal forgiveness. How does he start in this final breath of his life? How does he get there so he can move on and beyond? You can't undo the past. You can't go back in time and erase it. So, what to do? He didn't have much time left.

This is the ultimate riddle he realizes. The puzzle. The maze that he has to navigate so he may die in peace. In harmony. To enter the kingdom of the flow of it all, the universal energy, and then let go. But he cannot let go yet. Maybe that is why he has been lingering, to solve the mystery of self-forgiveness.

He tries his best to journey further back. To go back to the root of it all. He realizes that he has to go back to the very beginning in order to release himself at the very end. He feels like he has just a moment left. But in this world of the surreal and mystery, a moment could last a lifetime. He tries to squeeze his eyes tightly shut. He realizes that he has to let go now before he can finally let go and enter the world where it all began. He hopes he has enough time. He hopes he did not lose himself before he goes forever. So, he begins.

She is in the room alone now with her husband. Everyone has left her alone. Although they are close by . . . down the hall . . . in the "family lounge" or hospital cafe, it is just her energy next to his now, at the end. She realizes that she just plain loves him. He was flawed. They went through some bad times, yet she has loved him anyway.

Why? She shakes her head as if she is arguing with herself or trying to convince herself that life is just like that. Good. Bad. Pain. Joy. Forgiveness. Without forgiveness, there is just darkness. All the time. She doesn't want that.

Again she looks at him, this flawed human being, and she says to herself, "Okay . . . I admit it . . . I am flawed too. I have to take some of the weight and transfer it to my shoulders." And so, she does. And when she does this, it is as if lightness is entering the room. "I accept my role in this life too, my dear friend.

"I am not the total innocent one either. So maybe I have to forgive myself and you in this moment."

She takes his cold hand in her hands. She kissed it. She looks at his frail, broken body and only sees the boy he was. The boy she first met. The boy who stole her heart. The boy she gave her life story to. The boy she chose to travel through life with. The boy.

He feels a sudden release of stress and tension in his body. He feels peace flow over and through him. He feels forgiveness. He feels unconditional love. He feels in harmony with his wife and his surroundings. He then realizes that he can finally express himself.

He feels an awareness. He feels a sense of enlightenment. He realizes now he could journey to a place that will permit him to find clarity and comfort as he transitions over.

He decides to reflect, in these last few moments, on how to live a life of courage and nobility in a world that seems anything but courageous and noble. It is as if there is a pen in his hand. He begins to tell himself the lesson of life.

The lesson of his life. Maybe the lesson of life itself.

He hopes he has enough time. But he also knows that he has to hear it inside his head so that he can leave in peace. He begins the final chapter of his life.

He goes back to the very beginning.

He remembers when his mom told him the story of his birth. He had to be nine or ten when she sat him down and recounted how, on the day he was born . . . right after he was born, his heart stopped. The doctors and nurses yelled, "Code blue!" and began all type of life-saving procedures. But it was all for naught. He actually died on the day he was born.

His mom told him how she heartbroken was, and how his dad was devastated. As they were about to pronounce his death, however, his heart spontaneously began to beat again. A half hour had gone by and yet, somehow, some way, he was breathing and alive. His mom told him that the nurses told her that he was unique. The nurses all gathered together and prayed and thanked the Lord. They said he was a miracle baby.

From that day forward, after his mom related that story of his birth and death to him, life and death always fascinated him. It was part of the reason why the mystery of this journey both puzzled and amazed him. He understood that death was a heartbeat away from life and . . . well . . . you just never know what to expect.

For him, life began in death and he has now come full circle to death again. His heartbeat, which has lasted over six decades, initially only lasted six seconds. He feels as if it is the same now.

He is being reborn at the time of his death.

Maybe it will happen one more time. Maybe another miracle is in store for all of them.

Courage. He sees how this word is repeating itself on his final journey. Life and courage go hand in hand.

Although his body is slowly shutting down, he hopes that he has enough energy to go this final distance. He is not afraid. He has known this day would come again, but . . . *Why now?* If he could just learn the lesson and go on living!

It seems like a cruel joke to learn what he has learned and not be able to tell anyone or even use the knowledge in his daily life. Given the chance, he would live each day more fully. More honestly.

Over the years, he changed. The deaths of his loved ones caused him to be less critical. More understanding. It was as if the deaths were gifts in weird-shaped wrapping. The gifts were that of gladness to see a friend. Of not always being the critic of another. And the voices in his head were less noisy.

But here he is. Back with death. Like an old friend.

And so, the last lesson appears before him. The lesson of life and courage. The two go hand in hand. He moves his head slightly to the left. He cannot feel his fingers any longer. He senses his muscles relaxing. They are losing all texture and purpose. His mouth is getting dryer and dryer. His lips are chapped. His tongue feels swollen.

He hears his wife ask the nurse, "What is that sound?" The nurse matter-of-factly answers, "The death rattle."

"What is that? she asks.

The nurse replies, "It is the sound of fluid building up in his lungs."

He feels his bladder release urine. He is horrified. He realizes how helpless he is now. He feels ashamed although he understands that it is nature's way. And then his bowels empty whatever is left in him. He can smell it.

The nurse asks everyone to leave and for help from her aides to change him. Change him . . . like a newborn baby, but the other side of life.

The circle is closing in on him. He is dying again.

He knows that this was his last breath.

THE LAST BREATH

Courage is the ability to face difficulty with a brave heart. But how do we define *difficulty?* It comes in so many forms.

There can be physical difficulty. Illness, disease, crippling events either from birth or due to some accident.

Or emotional difficulty. Depression, anxiety, and stress can cripple a person's spirit.

Or mental or spiritual difficulty. There are so many ways we must summon courage. Maybe it is needed to face a normal day in a normal life in which we know our fate yet keep moving forward.

Maybe difficulty is just living life in all its stages and phases. Bad bosses. Cruel leaders, loud neighbors, troubled kids . . . the list of difficulties we face goes on and on.

A difficulty could be none of these. It could be merely the human condition. Being a frail being that constantly and foolishly seeks perfection is difficult. The images we are exposed to on TV and through social media drive so many of us to demand impossible criteria of themselves and their loved ones. To some, it feels like a constant losing game.

That's it, he realizes. *You need courage just to live life each day simply trying your best to be an authentic, genuine human being.*

Courage in the face of life itself.

Friends and loved ones live and die. Friends and loved ones get hurt and suffer. Life can be arbitrary. Life just is. Life doesn't choose sides. We think it does. But it doesn't. Life does not have to be fair. No one promised us that. Life can be a bouquet of roses with or without thorns, or both. It usually is both.

So, what are the choices we each have? To get lost in the truth itself that life is strange and odd since you expect that if you are good, good happens or you finally realize that stuff happens . . . good and bad . . . to good and bad people . . . and all you can do is have the courage to face the challenge that is life and play your hand . . . period.

Each day you choose to face the day's events with courage. To live heroically. To smile in the face of the reality that death awaits us all. And therefore, the ultimate challenge is living life itself with a brave heart and a soulful understanding that you are frail, fragile, easily broken and the response to all this has to be . . . *I*

*am here now. I matter now. I plant my flag in my life
right now and will live each moment as a courageous
warrior would live it.*

So, the key to life . . . this life . . . is to look up, look
out, seek the light, recognize that this one last breath is
the only breath we get. We don't need to seek approval
from others. We don't need to look outward for our
identity. We define ourselves and simply want to let
each one we care about find their own solid footing.
Only then can two whole people walk together. Only
then can children relax into learning about themselves.
Only then can you meet life on your terms and know
that in this one breath all of life exists and then dies.

He wants his wife not to mourn him. He wants her to
see him, flaws and all, and love him and then let him go.
He wants her to enjoy whatever time she has left with
no pain; only fond memories of a young boy who loved a
young girl . . . always.

He wants his daughter to forgive herself and know
that life is just so many random events crashing into
each other and she has to let go of self-torture. He wants
her to know that she is loved just as she is, and no one
is to blame. Life just happens.

He wants his brother to know that the saw accident
didn't change the essence of who he was. He was and is
a decent man who can live a full life and find love. The
what ifs are just that . . . what ifs. They mean and
signify nothing.

He wanted his dad to know that he was not a failure.
He wanted him to know that he was a hard-working guy

who loved his family and wanted to make the best out of anything thrown his way. He wasn't Willie Loman. He just tried to figure out how to live each day with the cards he was dealt. There is no shame in that. In fact, he was probably the most courageous of all the men he met in his life. His dad lived quietly and was just trying to find more parts of himself to express. All done in a basement and behind the steering wheel of a truck.

He wanted his mom to know that she was pure love. Unconditionally devoted to her family. No fancy bells and whistles about her. Just a decent woman who wanted to be as good a mom as she could be and who was beloved and is remembered just like that. Her death was from a broken dream. He wanted her to know that broken dreams didn't mean that she was broken.

He wanted his little girl to know that he thinks and dreams about her every day. There was not a day that went by that she was not alive in all his thoughts. Her death, as painful and avoidable as it was, taught them all a lesson. The lesson of forgiveness. The lesson of compassion. The lesson of passion for the slightest gift that is one moment in time. Time. Moments. Seconds. We are all here, and we all die. Why did that still surprise him and shock him so? So, in the end, it is not death that is the defining end of his life . . . rather, it was not living fully with the time until he died. His little girl taught him that life was to be shared. Embraced. Treasured. And that love must be shared. Always. And that this took courage.

IN THESE FIVE BREATHS

I am you. You are me. That is not trite. That is truth, he thinks.

He feels himself melting deeper into the hospital mattress. He is spent. *I am spent,* he thinks. That sounds odd since he has but one breath left. But that is how he feels. He has just enough energy now to go back to the mountain road and piece together his memories of the last moments before the accident. He wills himself back to the car. Back to the mountain. Back to the crash. Back to the whys and how-comes that brought him here to his deathbed.

He left the coffee shop and got in his car. He was intending on going home and taking a shower, chatting with his wife, calling his daughter to tell her he loved her. He did that nearly every morning. He would ask about his grandchildren and usually then would hear a few cute stories about the new things the little ones had done or said. That is what he intended to do.

As his car got to the turnoff to head home, he kept going straight. At first, he caught himself and was going to make a U-turn but then he didn't. He kept driving.

It was as if his whole life was coming together and converging on this ride up this mountain road. His mind was starting to fill with images. First of his little girl. Then of his dad. Then of his mom. His brother came into his consciousness. His brother's accident and how it changed his brother. Life with all its twists and turns.

He thought about how life was one huge Rube Goldberg machine. He thought how nothing seems to be direct in how it played out. Everything somehow indirectly affected or touched everything else, and in some complicated way, we end up where we are supposed to go all along. Many times, we do not even realize what dozen other direct and indirect, intended and unintended events occurred that got us from point A to point B.

A contraption. Life is one massive, intersecting, overlapping, contradicting contraption.

He was going to rush home to tell everyone he loved about his revelation. His awakening. Life was finally making some sense to him.

He saw that time is not linear. Life is not straight lines. It is not about the small story. It is not about the length of our time here but rather about the quality of our time here. Life unfolds. We all hang on as best we can. Life is about the mountainous story that binds us together . . . forever. The epic tale that is us here . . . now.

He was so excited by his discovery. An exhilaration filled him. He closed his eyes for a split second to give thanks . . . and it was then that he drifted.

His car hits the wall. His car careens over the edge. He realizes that he is at one of the steepest parts of the canyon. There are no guardrails. At first, the car is sliding down the side of the cliff. But as it gets steeper and more ragged, the car flips over and is now skidding through time and space. It flips two more times before coming to rest on the canyon floor. And it is now sitting in a river bed at the base of the canyon.

He had his seatbelt on. The airbag deployed. His arm and leg were broken in multiple paces as he slid down to the car's final resting place. The roof of the car was caved in, and his head was pinned to the side of his shoulder. His throat was basically cut off from all oxygen. He tried to twist and turn to get the air flowing back into his body, and he was partially successful, but it was not enough.

He felt aches and pains everywhere. He knew he had averted death for the moment, but that death was pounding on the car door. He was actually amazed he was still alive. The last thing he remembered before blacking out was looking around the car, hearing his wife's voice saying good morning to him, and then everything went dark. He passed out.

But that still doesn't answer the question of why he was on that road and not home with her. It was then that it hit him.

He was being airlifted out of the canyon. There were lights and sirens everywhere. He was now in an ambulance. She was with him. He sensed her being.

He heard her say, "What were you doing there?"

Although he couldn't talk, he heard himself say . . . *I needed to go higher up to be with them all. I needed to enter the silence. I needed to enter their presence undistracted from the noise of the day and of this life. They represent purity to me. They represent decency to me. I wanted to just sit with them one more time and tell them what they meant to me. I had to enter their world, so they knew it was okay to reenter mine. I wanted to sit with them all and for one last time be one with them.*

I wanted to sit with my mom on the car bumper in Lake George.

I wanted to sit with my dad in the basement and watch him paint. I wanted my dad to know he mattered . . . to me.

I wanted to be with our little angel and hear her giggle one more time.

And . . . I did!

They wouldn't let me die until we had these moments of grace. They needed to tell me one more tale and walk together with me one more time.

Honey, I went up, so I could come back to you whole again. I am here now . . . bruised and beaten up a bit by life . . . but finally whole.

Maybe it takes a lifetime, no matter how short or long, to become whole. The world has a way of taking its toll on us all. We can be quite battered around by events, circumstances, choices, decisions, and the needs, criticisms, demands and expectations of other people. Sometimes we are battered around by the inner voices and demons that come to visit us all from time to time. But then, in the end . . . the clouds part. The chatter subsides. The clarity fights its way through. The perfection of this imperfect existence . . . this improbable journey . . . shows itself for what it is. A gift. A bit tattered and roughed up and yet a gift nevertheless.

Breath. The ultimate gift that we completely take for granted. *Or maybe,* he thinks, *we cheat ourselves by naming it "breath."* Would it all be different if we named it "life." Life. Taking life in moment by moment.

It seems so obvious now. If he could only let her know!

Moment-by-moment living.

And then . . . he finds himself in the hospital bed with just one breath left. With his eyes closed and his mind clear, he knows it is now finally time to let go. He is calm and more content that he has ever been before. He gives an internal nod to himself.

We have this choice in the end. Are we good with the story we told throughout our days? Flaws and all. Blemishes and all.

Life is not for the weak and timid. Life is for the courageous and bold . . . and kind souls.

My love . . . I hope you have a long and joyful life. I hope you find peace. You are loved. Don't mourn me. When you think of me . . . smile and say, "Oh, my sweet boy . . . please . . ."

He releases the last breath. His life. He releases his life. He feels himself let go.

Then he sees a bright light. He is walking through a dark tunnel, and the light at the far end is getting brighter and brighter. And now he is surrounded by the white light. He feels loved. He feels secure. He feels like he is home.

She is standing over him as he lets his life go. She knows it was the last piece of himself. She knows he is gone. It is odd, but she thinks she sees a glow come over him. She thinks she actually sees a smile come over his face. It is as if he has walked into the house after a good day and is being embraced by his family.

She kisses his lips and says, "Good night, sweet boy. And thank you. For everything."

After the Last Breath

As she walks out of the room, the nurse walks in and pulls the sheet over his face. The nurse pauses for a moment. She comments to herself that he looks so at peace.

One more person, in one more hospital on one more Wednesday night exits the stage of life. And what a life. It has had all the love, heartbreak, joy, sadness and excitement that one life should and could have. No one can tell how long they will live, but each can have a say in how much life is in the years that they do live.

The nurse turns to her aide and says, "He seemed like a nice guy. What a sweet family. I wonder what he was doing on that mountain road. What a freak accident."

Then she says, "We have to get the room ready. There is a patient coming up from emergency with a gunshot wound." And so, it goes.

She walks to her car. Her daughter meets her outside.
His brother catches up with them. Both had gone into
his room before he was wheeled out and said a prayer
over him. His daughter leaned over his ear and said,
"Please take care of my baby sister. Tell her I love her
so and miss her every day."

His brother touched his arm, smiled, and said, "Bye,
buddy," then he looked down and walked out of the
room.

Outside in the parking lot, they hug each other.

She says, "We have so much to do. But let's not do
morbid things. Let's have a celebration instead. He
always liked parties. Let's toast him and our family.
None of us get out of life alive, so let's not mourn the
inevitable. Let's celebrate a life well lived." She lets out
the biggest laugh.

They both look at her. What, they ask, is she
laughing about on this cold, sad Wednesday night?

She tells them, "He was right all along. It is the
moments in between that count. And his moments
counted. Our life together mattered. We counted."

Then she hugs them again and says she'll see them
tomorrow. "Get some rest."

She gets in her car and sits quietly for a moment. It
is over. This story is done. The book in the sky is
closing its last page on this one soul. All those years
together! She thinks back to their first kiss. The first
time they made love. She can't believe all the decades

that have passed. Time is such a trickster. And the river keeps flowing. Other stories will now be told.

It feels like it was just yesterday. And maybe it was. Maybe it is all an illusion. A drop of rain containing their life story is now evaporating into the ether. So many raindrops. So many stories.

She turns on the ignition and tunes the radio to an oldies station. As she drives off, leaving the hospital parking lot, the song comes on . . . their song . . . That first date.

Johnny Mathis' "The Twelfth of Never." She hopes he knew how much she loved him. She nods to herself. He did.

The night engulfs her car as she turns onto Route 119 and heads home.

Epilogue

He opens his eyes and finds himself in an open field. He is lying in tall grass and can feel sunlight on his face.

There is no one else in sight. He is alone in a veritable field of dreams. It seems like a Sunday afternoon. The sun is bright, and the breeze warmly embraces him. He has never felt so good. Unbroken. Whole.

He stands up and looks around, then senses a presence.

He can see some people walking toward him. He cannot quite make them out at first. Then he sees her . . . A young child has started running toward him. Her arms are reaching out to him. He reaches out his arms for her. They embrace in the open field. As they hold each other tightly, joyously, he senses the others gathering around him. They are welcoming him home.

It is a good day to be alive.

ACKNOWLEDMENTS

After *Hour of the Wolf,* I waited years until the moment arrived to write *In These Five Breaths.* I needed inspiration to tell this tale of life, love, loss, redemption, and atonement.

This writing was not possible without the love and understanding of my wife, Margie. I am eternally grateful to her.

I also want to thank all my friends and family who kept asking when the "next" book was coming out.

My daughters, Melissa and Lindsay, are a constant blessing and my grandchildren, Ryan, Reghan, and Hunter, are my constant teachers.

My sons-in-law, Mason and Brad, remind me of the constant road we are traveling to find meaning in this unfolding journey.

My mom and dad, Lorraine and Maurice, are forever with me. I miss them every day.

My sister, Heather, brother-in-law and sister-in-law, Harold and Sue, are unconditionally present as the road is walked by us all.

Finally, I would like to thank my book editor, Stephanie Gunning, her assistant, Najat Washington, and the cover designer, Gus Yoo, for their wonderful work and support.

We are mere visitors on the earth. Temporary occupants. Please stay connected with those who matter.

Breath is life.

ABOUT THE AUTHOR

Paul R. Lipton is an attorney, author, and speaker. His previous book is *Hour of the Wolf: An Experiment in Ageless Living.*

As an attorney, Paul tried cases for more than forty years. Paul began his career as an assistant district attorney in Nassau County, New York, before moving to Florida. Once there, he practiced law in a number of law firms. For thirteen years, he was a trial attorney with the international law firm of Greenberg Traurig. He retired from the active practice of law and currently is Director of Professionalism, Career, and Skill Development at the law firm of Rumberger Kirk & Caldwell. Paul is a frequent speaker to various business and professional organizations, addressing topics such as finding a balanced life in a professional and business world that seems out of balance and finding your moral compass in the uncharted territory of demands being made just to get the result no matter the consequences.

As an undergraduate, Paul attended Penn State University, where he was a member of the history, political science, and social science honor societies. Paul then attended Washington University School of Law, where he was a note editor for the *Urban Law Annual*.

Paul has been married to Margie since 1968. They have two beautiful daughters, Melissa and Lindsay, and two sons-in-law, Mason and Brad. Paul and Margie also have three wonderful grandchildren, Ryan, Reghan, and Hunter.

A longtime resident of Miami, Florida, Paul now resides in Boulder, Colorado.